"We c

Cassidy had managed to pull the skylight open as wide as it would go. There was just enough room to stick her head in and get a good look at the horse. He was a chestnut, the same size as Pizzazz, with identical markings. *But something about the way this horse carried himself was just different — the way people had different mannerisms,* Cassidy thought. He might look like Pizzazz on the outside, but he wasn't Pizzazz on the inside. She took one last look and then took her head out of the opening. Then suddenly, she understood why the other horse was in the trailer.

"You guys, I know what's going on!" Cassidy said. "They must have known Pizzazz wouldn't pass the track vet's exam! So they got this other horse that looks identical to him, and they let the track vet examine him instead! No one noticed the switch. Except us," she added, pushing the skylight back to half-closed. She began to climb down from the top of the truck. "All we have to do is go tell all those reporters and everyone will know about it! We can stop the race!"

Collect all the books in the THOROUGHBRED series:

THOROUGHBRED Super Editions

ASHLEIGH'S Thoroughbred Collection

*coming soon

THOROUGHBRED

CASSIDY'S SECRET

CREATED BY
JOANNA CAMPBELL

WRITTEN BY
ALLISON ESTES

HarperEntertainment
A Division of HarperCollinsPublishers

HarperEntertainment
A Division of HarperCollins*Publishers*
10 East 53rd Street, New York, NY 10022-5299

This is a work of fiction. The characters, incidents, and dialogues are products of the author's imagination and are not to be construed as real. Any resemblance to actual events or persons, living or dead, is entirely coincidental.

Produced by 17th Street Productions, a division of Daniel Weiss Associates, Inc.

HarperCollins books are available at special quantity discounts for bulk purchases for sales promotions, premiums, or fund-raising. For information please write: Special Markets Department, HarperCollins Publishers, Inc., 10 East 53rd Street, New York, NY 10022-5299.

ISBN 0-06-106543-9

First printing: January 1999

Printed in the United States of America

Visit HarperEntertainment on the World Wide Web at
http://www.harpercollins.com

❖ 10 9 8 7 6 5 4 3 2 1

1

IN THE MAIN RING AT GARDENER FARM, FOUR RIDERS SAT ON
their horses under a shady overhang of oak branches
heavy with acorns. The Indian-summer sunshine had
mellowed, turning the late afternoon light into a golden
haze, but it was still warm enough for both horses and
riders to be grateful for the shade. The horses stood
sleepily, motionless except for the steady swishing of
their tails and an occasional toss of a head. The riders,
three girls and a boy, were watching a fifth rider canter
down one side of the arena toward a jump.

The cantering rider was Cassidy Smith, a tall, slender girl with two wings of blond hair showing under
the sides of her helmet. She was riding a big bay horse,
and both the brown eyes of the horse and the green eyes
of the girl were riveted on the jump ahead of them.

"Three, two, one," Cassidy chanted aloud as she

1

approached the fence. Just as she said "one," she felt her Canadian Warmblood jumper, Rebound, lift his front legs and leap smartly over the crossed, yellow rails of the Swedish oxer. *Great,* Cassidy thought. *We found the perfect distance to that jump.*

"Good, Cassidy," Mona agreed. Mona Gardener, the owner of Gardener Farm, stood in the middle of the arena. Her short brown hair was hidden under a baseball cap, and her skinny legs were deeply tanned under her khaki cargo shorts. She took several purposeful steps in time with Rebound's strides as Cassidy cantered past her. "Now count down your strides before the stone wall," Mona instructed. Then she stopped and placed her hands on her hips in her characteristic "let's see you do it" stance.

Cassidy nodded her head once at Mona to indicate that she understood, then moved her right leg back slightly, pressing it into Rebound's side. At the same time, she shifted her left hand to guide him in a smooth turn to the wooden jump painted to look like a stone wall. She kept her eye on the jump as Rebound's strides brought her closer and closer to it. The wall itself was only about two-feet high. Mona had set two blue rails above it, raising the height to three feet, but that was still low for Cassidy and Rebound. She had ridden the shiny, dark bay gelding in the Junior Jumpers at many big, A-rated horse shows, where the height of the fences was usually three feet, six inches, or three feet, nine inches.

Cassidy was more advanced than the four other kids

in the class, so Mona had asked her to demonstrate the exercise, which was to count down the strides before a jump. In fact, Cassidy reflected, it seemed like Mona was always asking her to go first. Sometimes Cassidy wished she wouldn't. It wasn't that she minded going first, but the way Mona was always pointing her out as a good example made her feel like she stood out from the other kids, just when she was trying her hardest to fit in.

"I want you guys to watch how Cassidy uses her eyes," Mona said to the other kids.

Cassidy barely heard the comment. She was too busy concentrating on the exercise, which was supposed to help a rider learn to judge the distance to the take-off spot before a jump. It was a familiar exercise, one she'd done many times with her old trainer down in Florida, but it was also a fun one, so today she didn't mind being the guinea pig.

When she felt she was three strides from the stone wall, Cassidy counted aloud again, "Three, two, one." On the "one," Rebound rocked back on his haunches and neatly cleared the fence, snapping his knees right up to his chin.

"Excellent," Mona said.

Cassidy rode a few strides away from the jump, then brought Rebound to a walk. He came down willingly, but walked quickly, with his ears flicking eagerly forward and back, as if he were just waiting for Cassidy to point him at the next fence.

Cassidy laughed and patted his sleek, dark neck.

"That's it, Rebound, you jumped them all. Now it's somebody else's turn."

Rebound let out a disappointed-sounding snort, then lowered his head and relaxed into a quiet walk. Cassidy held the reins by the buckle, casually guiding the horse with one hand toward the shady spot where the other riders were waiting.

"Okay, who wants to go next?" Mona asked, looking expectantly at her students.

Dylan Becker, the only boy, spoke first. "I will," he said quickly, shortening the reins of his appendix quarter-horse, Dakota, and turning him away from the group toward the middle of the arena. "Nice riding, Cassidy," he said appreciatively as he passed her.

"Thanks," Cassidy replied, smiling with pleasure. If there was one person besides Mona whose opinion really mattered to her, it was Dylan. Cassidy had just moved to Kentucky that summer, and though she'd tried her best to be friendly, the girls had been difficult to get to know. It was Dylan who had been her first friend.

"That was really good," Christina Reese said. Christina, twelve, was tall for her age, and just as good a rider as Cassidy, though not as experienced.

"Thanks," Cassidy said. She was glad that she and Christina were getting along much better since school had started. The two hadn't exactly hit it off when they first met.

"You sure make it look easy," Melanie Graham, Christina's cousin agreed. Melanie was from New York.

She was a few months older than her cousin, but she was tiny, with short, pale blond hair and large, sad brown eyes. Cassidy had decided that she really liked Melanie, maybe because they were both newcomers.

"We've done this one a lot, haven't we, Rebound?" Cassidy stroked her horse's neck which was damp and shiny with sweat. She kicked her feet out of the stirrups and let herself slouch in the saddle. The shade felt great; she could feel her pulse pounding in her temples and she knew her face would be flushed bright-red from the ride.

"Rebound looks like so much fun to ride," Katie Garrity said. Thirteen-year-old Katie was Christina's best friend, but she was always friendly to Cassidy. "He always looks all happy and bouncy, like a big puppy."

"He *is* a big puppy," Cassidy said, grinning.

"I just hope Sterling starts to like jumping as much as Rebound seems to," Christina said.

Christina was riding her four-year-old Thorough-bred, Sterling Dream, who at that moment was the only one of the five horses who didn't look half asleep. Sterling pawed nervously at a patch of grass she had been cropping, then shifted sideways, switching her tail rapidly from side to side.

"What's the matter with her?" Melanie asked. Melanie was sitting on her cousin's outgrown pony, a pretty, rotund, black-and-white pinto named Tribula-tion. "Hey, watch it!" she protested, as Sterling backed into the pony in her agitation.

Trib, who'd been half asleep, opened his eyes in alarm and scooted forward. Melanie hauled back on the reins, but they were too long, and she ended up trotting along the fence for several yards before she shortened them enough to stop him. "Whoa, Trib," she commanded. It came out sounding like "whoa-oa-oa, Tri-i-ib" because Trib was trotting so fast Melanie that was bouncing all over the place.

Cassidy and Katie couldn't help laughing. Christina was giggling, too, though she was still trying to get Sterling to settle down.

"Sorry, Mel," Christina called. "It's the flies. They're driving Sterling nuts."

Melanie had managed to get Trib turned around. He headed reluctantly back toward the group. "Didn't you put fly-spray on her?" Melanie asked.

Sterling stomped a hind foot impatiently and then stood still. Christina shook her head. "I forgot. Sorry, Sterling," she murmured, patting the mare's dark, dappled neck.

Melanie had finally convinced Trib that it was okay to rejoin the group, but the pony's ears were still on alert, and he kept a watchful eye on Sterling.

"Boy, the flies are terrible," Cassidy said.

"It's the heat," Katie agreed.

"It's supposed to be fall," Melanie said. "Is it always this hot in Kentucky this time of year?"

"Not usually," Christina said. "But we had an unusually warm spring, too."

6

"I hope it means we're going to have a mild winter," Katie said. "Remember last winter, that big snowstorm we had?"

"I was sort of hoping that it would snow," Cassidy said. "I've never lived in a place where you have real winter weather. My parents took me and my brothers skiing once, but that was such a long time ago." Cassidy paused, remembering the trip. She'd been about six or seven years old. It was one of the few times she could remember her family ever going anyplace together. "That's the only time I ever saw snow," she said wistfully.

"How'd you like it?" Melanie asked.

"I thought it was great!" Cassidy said.

"Well, you're bound to see some snow this winter, even if we are having an extra dose of summer," Katie assured her.

"I didn't know you had brothers," Christina said curiously. "Are they older or younger?"

"Well, my oldest brother, Carter, is in college," Cassidy told them. "In pre-med. He's twenty. And Campbell, my other brother is three years older than me; he's sixteen."

"What does your dad do?" Katie asked.

Cassidy hesitated. So far she had managed to avoid telling the other kids much of anything about her family and how they had ended up in Kentucky. Even Dylan didn't know the whole story. "He, um . . . he sells insurance . . ." she offered. She wondered what they

7

would think if she told them that her father, Harrison Smith, had been a trainer of Thoroughbreds in Miami. Had been. But that was before they'd had to move—before—

"Okay, who's next?" Mona interrupted Cassidy's thoughts, and the conversation.

"I'll go," Christina said. "Maybe the flies won't catch us if we keep moving." As she nudged Sterling forward she gave Cassidy a curious look. Cassidy hoped Christina wouldn't ask any more questions later.

Dylan was walking Dakota toward them, patting the horse's neck affectionately.

Christina smiled sweetly at him. "You looked great, Dylan," she told him as she rode past.

"It *felt* great," Dylan said, sounding very satisfied with Dakota's performance.

"Are you sure you wouldn't rather be out riding dirt bikes with Chad?" Melanie teased.

"Positive," Dylan said. "That's Katie's job," he added.

Katie blushed. Cassidy knew Chad Walker from Dylan's soccer team. She knew that Katie and Chad had been a couple at one time, but she hadn't known that they were an "item" again.

"Hey, did you see what happened?" Melanie said to Dylan. "This fly was bothering Sterling, and—"

"There's too much talking going on over there," Mona said pointedly. "Have respect for the rider on course." Though they had all been chatting, Mona had directed her comment to Melanie.

Melanie looked miffed, but she closed her mouth. Cassidy wasn't at all surprised to hear Mona reprimand them. David, her old instructor in Miami, would have said the same thing, but a lot more strongly. *In fact, he would probably have yelled,* Cassidy reflected. That was one of the good things about Mona. She never raised her voice.

They stood quietly now, watching Christina ride through the course, counting down the strides. Cassidy expected to see Sterling rush. She had ridden Sterling a few times over the summer when Christina's wrist was broken and knew that if anything was bothering the mare, she was likely to be tense and quick. But maybe Sterling was just glad to leave the flies behind. She stayed calm and collected through the whole course, only rushing the last jump.

Cassidy watched Christina collect the mare with some firm half halts and bring her down to a walk. Christina listened intently to Mona's comments, then walked back to the shade tree.

"She's really settling down," Cassidy complimented Christina as she rejoined the group. "That looked great."

"Thanks," Christina said frowning, "but the last jump was terrible."

"It's always tough jumping toward the in-gate," Cassidy offered. "Especially when you're riding a horse that tends to be quick anyway. I bet if you jumped it again, you'd be ready for it, and then you could keep her slowed down."

Christina seemed to be digesting this information. Cassidy hoped she was taking it as a compliment, as she had intended. She had learned to be careful of what she said to Christina, who sometimes took things the wrong way. When Cassidy and Christina first met, Christina had had a huge crush on Dylan and thought that Cassidy was interested in him, too. Cassidy had tried to let Christina know that she didn't feel that way about him at all; she and Dylan were just really good friends, but she felt like she had to keep reassuring Christina of that fact.

"Cassidy's right, Chris," Dylan commented. "Sterling looked beautiful. You both did," he added, flashing Christina his best smile. He held out his hand to Christina as if he were giving her a high-five, but instead of a quick slap, they clasped hands for a moment, gazing intently at each other.

Cassidy had to look away. Watching Dylan and Christina reminded her of Jamie Santiago, her boyfriend in Miami. A lot of things about moving had been hard to take; losing Jamie had been one of the worst. She pictured Jamie's dark hair and sparkling dark eyes, his wide smile showing all his white teeth in his tan face. She remembered the feel of his arms around her and how stricken he had looked when she had to tell him she was leaving. *Stop it,* she scolded herself. She bit her lip hard to keep it from trembling and concentrated on watching Katie jump around the course on Seabreeze. "Three, two, one," she whispered, trying to time the countdown with Seabreeze's strides.

Seabreeze jumped the little course almost lazily. Katie had no trouble counting out all the distances. By the time Katie got to the last jump, Cassidy had managed to push the picture of Jamie back where it belonged, with the other memories of Miami that she wished she could forget but knew she never would.

After Katie's round, they had to wait while Mona lowered the fences six inches for Melanie. Trib could jump three feet easily, but Melanie wasn't quite ready for it. "Last but not least," Mona said to Melanie, when she had finished setting down the fences.

Cassidy watched as Melanie picked up a canter and started for the first fence. Melanie, she knew, did most of her riding over at Whitebrook Farm, where she lived with Christina and Christina's parents. They owned and ran Whitebrook, a large Thoroughbred training and breeding farm. Melanie worked as a pony girl, leading the high-spirited racers to and from the barns for their workouts. She rode a big black Thoroughbred gelding named Pirate, an ex-racehorse who was almost completely blind. *She's really getting better*, Cassidy thought, as Melanie jumped the first jump smoothly.

"Melanie, count," Mona urged her. Melanie had been concentrating so hard on the jump that she had forgotten the exercise. "Three, two, one," Mona said, timing the count to the next fence to help Melanie get the idea.

"Three, two, one . . ." Melanie chanted as she approached the third jump. But when she said "one,"

11

Trib was still a whole stride away from the jump. "Um . . . zero!" she added, as Trib sensibly waited to jump until he was close enough to the fence.

Cassidy and the other kids laughed. At the last jump, the little wall, Melanie waited until she was closer before she started counting. "Three, two—uh-oh!" she said, as Trib jumped the fence on "two." Luckily Melanie had grabbed a handful of mane, so she didn't get too badly left behind as Trib cleared the fence.

"Well, that was interesting," Mona remarked, as Melanie cantered away from the wall and brought Trib around in a little circle at a trot before slowing him to a walk.

"Oops," Melanie said. She giggled sheepishly. "Guess I need to practice that one some more."

"You need to focus on staying still and steady in two-point position," Mona told her. "Then you'll start getting a better feel for the distances. When you change your position so much, you never develop any consistency. Try practicing lots of transitions while you stay in two-point," Mona suggested.

"You're really improving, Melanie," Cassidy said encouragingly as Melanie rejoined the group under the shade tree.

"You've got to be kidding," Melanie said rolling her eyes. "That was horrible."

"Well, you had a little trouble with the counting part but you looked good over the jumps," Katie said helpfully.

"I'm thinking of writing a book on riding," Melanie said. "It'll be called *Melanie Graham's Bizarre Jumping Style.*"

"Why don't you just call it, *Hanging On For Dear Life?*" Christina suggested.

"No, I've got it," Melanie said. "*Grunt-Seat Equitation.*"

They all had a good chuckle over Melanie's spoof on the title of a popular book on hunt-seat equitation. Cassidy was glad to be laughing for a change.

"We all get left behind sometimes," Dylan said, when they had calmed down.

"You really are getting better, Mel," Cassidy added.

"The next time will be easier. You'll see," Katie agreed.

"There's one good thing about doing really badly the first time you try something. You've got nowhere to go but up!" Melanie joked.

"You know, that's true," Christina remarked. "Sometimes I wish Sterling and I hadn't won our first event."

"Why?" Katie asked incredulously.

"I'd be so psyched if I won an event," Dylan said. "I was happy winning fourth place. If I came in first I'd be going crazy!"

"But when you start off with a blue ribbon, and then you don't win anything the next time, it's kind of hard to take," Christina pointed out. "You feel like you're getting worse instead of better."

"But you know that's not true," Mona said. She had

13

come over to the group of riders and was listening to their conversation. "It was great that you and Sterling won that horse trial. Think what it did to build your confidence."

"Yeah, remember how you were so worried about getting back on her after you broke your wrist?" Cassidy reminded her.

"Yeah, but I feel like we work and work and we're stuck at the same level," Christina complained. "Sterling still hates to jump water, she still rushes the fences sometimes, and—"

"Sterling's young, Christina," Mona said. "You have to remember that. You're also still schooling the racehorse out of her. Look at the big picture. Sterling always hated water, but now you've got her jumping it and walking through it. She may not like it, but she's getting used to it. In time, she'll settle down even more. She's not rushing the fences as much as she used to, either. It's frustrating to have those bad moments, because you're getting more and more good ones."

"Mona's right," Cassidy agreed. "Sterling is getting better. I can see it."

"I wish I could," Christina grumbled. "You're lucky," she said to Cassidy. "Rebound is the perfect jumper."

Cassidy started to protest, then realized there was nothing she could say. Rebound really was great. And she was lucky to have him. "He just loves to jump," she agreed, finally. "And he's the kind of horse who's always eager to please."

"Sterling's really trying, Christina," Mona said. "She just has a lot of doubt to overcome."

"That's one of the best things about horses," Dylan remarked. "How they trust you and try to please you, however hard it may be."

"That's right," Mona said quietly. "It's called 'heart.' Heart is what makes a great horse. Not size or speed or jumping ability. Not perfect legs or a perfectly angled shoulder. Not breeding or looks or temperament. Heart is what wins the race or jumps the jump or crosses the stream," she said, looking pointedly at Christina. "Sterling has heart. All these horses do," Mona said. She gazed at each horse and rider, seeming to gather them in with her clear gray eyes. "Never forget that. And be careful how you use it. Heart is what makes a horse die trying."

All the kids were silent, as the meaning of Mona's words settled upon them. Mona had been talking to all of them, but Cassidy had the uneasy feeling that maybe Mona knew about what had happened in Miami. She hoped not. *If she did, would it change Mona's opinion of her?* She looked worriedly at Mona, trying to guess what she might be thinking, but Mona's eyes were unreadable.

Cassidy began to feel more and more uncomfortable. She wished somebody would say something. Then suddenly Sterling let out a squeal of indignation and launched herself straight into the air.

15

2

"Oh!" Cassidy said, startled.

Sterling leaped into the air a second time, kicking out with her hind feet before she landed again. Christina was thrown forward, but she quickly managed to sit up. "Whoa!" she commanded firmly.

"Yikes," Melanie exclaimed, as Trib let out a startled grunt and bolted down the fence line for the second time that day.

"Melanie, sit up and shorten your reins!" Mona told her, with a quick glance at Sterling.

"Uh-oh," Cassidy said, watching Trib gallop around the corner at the far end of the ring.

"Oh my gosh, he's totally running away with her," Katie said, her blue eyes round with alarm.

"Melanie, pulley rein!" Mona called, hurrying

16

toward the center of the ring where Melanie would be able to hear her better.

Cassidy heard Mona calling out further instructions to Melanie, but she had to keep an eye on Sterling. The mare was dancing around, snorting, and tossing her head in an annoyed manner.

"What's the matter with her?" Dylan asked, as Dakota snorted in fear and shied away from the frantic horse.

"I don't know," Christina said anxiously, struggling with the reins, trying to get Sterling to stand still.

What was bothering the mare? Cassidy tried, but she couldn't see anything wrong from where she was watching. Then she had to move Rebound out of the way as Sterling began to hop around in a circle of bucks that grew bigger and bigger as the horse grew more and more frantic.

"Look, Sterling's got a big horsefly on her leg!" Katie exclaimed.

"Where?" Christina said.

"Ohmigosh, it's huge," Katie said, backing Seabreeze away from Sterling.

"Where is it?" Christina asked. Sterling stopped bucking for a moment and cow-kicked with one hind leg toward her belly, trying to dislodge the horsefly.

"I see it," Cassidy said. "It's right there on the inside of her leg."

"Somebody help," Christina pleaded, as Sterling

executed another energetic leap into the air.

Cassidy glanced over at Mona, who was still busy trying to help Melanie get Trib under control. "Hang on, I'll get it," Cassidy said to Christina. She quickly dismounted and took the reins over Rebound's head so that she could hold on to him while she tried to help Christina. Cautiously she approached Sterling, who was still dancing around.

"Cassidy, be careful," Dylan cautioned her.

Cassidy dodged another cow-kick, then made a carefully timed swat at the horsefly with her hand. It dropped to the ground and lay in the dirt, stunned. Cassidy was going to stomp it, but Sterling beat her to it. She stamped a front foot angrily and that was the end of the fly. Then Sterling let out an indignant snort, as if she were making sure everyone knew just how she felt about horseflies. Everybody laughed.

"Thanks, Cassidy," Christina said, sounding genuinely grateful.

"Thank Sterling," Cassidy said smiling. Relieved, she noticed that Melanie had finally gotten Trib to stop. He was standing in the middle of the ring, panting. Mona had a hand on the reins and was saying something earnestly to Melanie.

Rebound stood alert but calm through the whole incident. "Good boy," Cassidy murmured, stroking his neck.

"Oooh, Christina, she's bleeding," Katie said, pointing to Sterling's leg.

A trickle of bright-red blood creeping down the inside of Sterling's left thigh showed where the fly had bitten her. Christina dismounted and bent down to examine the bite. "Poor Sterling," she lamented.

"Is everybody okay?" Mona was approaching them, leading Trib and Melanie. Trib's eyes still looked wild, with the whites showing at the corners, and Melanie's face was pale instead of red. "What was that all about?" she asked, raising an eyebrow at Sterling, who was standing quietly as if the whole event had never happened.

"It was a horsefly," Cassidy explained.

"I see," Mona said. "Now I could be mistaken, but I think I heard of little invention that would help with this sort of problem. It's called fly-spray," Mona quipped.

Christina looked sheepish. "I know, I know, I should've put it on her. It's just, I was halfway down to the ring when I remembered it, and—"

"And nothing," Mona said. "You shouldn't have forgotten it in the first place," she chided her. "And when you did remember, you should have gone back for it. You know how sensitive she is." Mona gestured with her head at Sterling.

"I know," Christina said humbly. "Sorry. I won't forget it again."

"I'm sure you won't," Mona said. She looked at Melanie. "You look a little pale there, Mel. You're not going to drop on me are you?" she joked.

"Man, I think Trib could be a racehorse," Melanie

said. "I had no idea he could go that fast."

"Oh, he's fast all right," Christina assured her. She eyed her old partner critically. "But you know something? He used to be faster. I think he's slowing down a little in his old age."

At that moment, Trib shook his head emphatically and let out a snort.

"I guess he has a different opinion about that," Mona said.

"Don't give him any ideas, Christina, please," Melanie begged. "He's plenty fast enough for me."

"All right, you guys," Mona said, glancing at her watch. "You've tortured me enough for one day. Go hose off these horses and put them away. And, Christina, make sure you put something on that fly bite," Mona added.

"I will," Christina promised.

Mona left the ring through the in-gate and hiked up the path to the barn. The kids ran up their stirrups, loosened the girths, and trudged up the hill after her, leading their horses.

Up at the barn, Cassidy quickly untacked Rebound and led him around to the side of the barn where there were two outdoor washracks for hosing horses in hot weather. Christina was already there, hosing off Sterling, with Melanie standing nearby, letting Trib graze.

20

"Mind if we join you in a bath?" Cassidy asked, leading Rebound to the second washrack.

"Come on in," Christina said, spraying Sterling's neck. "I'm almost done with the hose."

The washracks were like small stalls enclosed by metal rails. Each one had a concrete slab floor with a drain in the middle. Cassidy led her horse into the second washrack and waited for Christina to finish with the hose.

Cassidy was curious. "How come you're hosing her here, instead of when you get home?" she asked. Cassidy boarded her horses at Gardener Farm, but Melanie and Christina rode over from Whitebrook for their lessons. It was only about a mile, whether they went by the main road or cut through Mona's back pasture, which bordered the pastures of Whitebrook.

"It's getting dark earlier now," Christina explained. "If I wait until we get back home to hose her, she'll still be wet at feeding time. This way she's almost dry by the time we get home. Then all I have to do is feed her and rub off the saddle marks with a towel." She handed the hose to Cassidy. "Here."

"Thanks." Cassidy turned the hose on Rebound's legs to get him used to the water before she moved the hose up, wetting his chest and sides.

Christina picked up a sweat scraper and began scraping the excess water off Sterling's body. Sterling's dark skin showed through her wet, gray coat, making her look like she was dipped in silver. Cassidy couldn't help admiring the mare. In spite of her unpredictable temperament, she was a beautiful animal. There was something about her, a sort of star quality that made her stand out from other horses, that made you want to look at her. *Like Lady T*, Cassidy reflected.

Lady T was a racehorse—at the moment, a very famous racehorse. That spring Lady T had distinguished herself by winning three very prestigious stakes races for fillies: the Acorn, the Mother Goose, and the Oaks. Only four other horses had ever won "the Filly Triple Crown," so Lady T's wins had made headlines all over the country.

"Melanie, you're letting him graze way too much," Christina admonished. "He's still hot."

Melanie tugged at the reins and Trib agreeably lifted his head, munching a mouthful of grass. But as soon as he swallowed the mouthful, he plunged his face into the grass again, nearly yanking Melanie off her feet. "Hey," she protested, struggling to get his head up. The pony plowed a few steps forward, dragging Melanie along as he snatched the grass in greedy mouthfuls.

"Melanie, get his head up!" Christina cautioned her.

"I'm trying!" Melanie protested, giving a mighty pull on the reins.

"Here. Bring him into the washrack." Christina led Sterling out to make room for Trib. Melanie finally got Trib's head out of the grass again and managed to drag him into the washrack. He stood resigned, gazing hungrily at the grass that he could no longer reach.

22

Cassidy finished washing Rebound. She passed the hose to Melanie, who began spraying Trib right in the face.

"Melanie!" Christina said. "You're supposed to start with their feet. What are you doing?"

Cassidy watched to see how Melanie would respond. Melanie was less experienced around horses, so she had to take a certain amount of criticism from Christina. But Cassidy had learned that Melanie's independent streak would kick in at some point, and she would let Christina know that she'd had enough.

"I know how you're supposed to do it," Melanie said confidently. "Trib likes this, though, don't you Trib?" She directed the cool spray on the pony's broad, white forehead. His eyes were squeezed shut and his ears were flat back, but he really did seem to be enjoying it. He turned his lips out in a monkey-face and tossed his head playfully as the water streamed over him. "See?" Melanie said triumphantly.

"Well, don't get it in his ears," Christina grumbled. "And hurry up. We have to get home."

"What for? It's Friday night. Let's go to a movie." Katie was approaching, leading Seabreeze, whose dark brown coat looked as slick and shiny as a seal's. Dylan was right behind her with Dakota. They had used the wash stall in the barn to hose down their horses. Seabreeze and Dakota didn't waste a second. They dropped their heads to the grass and began munching happily.

"Great idea!" Melanie said. Then she yawned hugely. "Wow. If I can stay awake."

"I thought you were the big partier from New York City," Dylan kidded her. "Don't tell me they go to bed this early up there."

"I don't see you getting up at five o'clock in the morning, soccer boy," Melanie retorted. "I have a job, you know."

"Oh, yeah. How many more hours do you have to work before Pirate is yours?" Cassidy asked. She knew Melanie's aunt and uncle had promised Melanie she could "buy" Pirate Treasure by working as a pony girl. But it meant that Melanie had to get up early and pony several horses each morning before school. Cassidy admired Melanie's dedication. She wasn't sure she'd be able to stick to such a demanding schedule.

"I figure by the end of December, he should be all mine." Melanie grinned. "Then I can start charging Uncle Mike for my expert ponying skills."

"So who wants to go to the movies?" Katie prodded.

"I do," Christina said. "But I'll have to check with Mom."

"I'll try," Melanie said, yawning again.

"Cassidy?" Dylan said.

"I can't," Cassidy said.

"Why not?" Melanie demanded.

"I . . . There's something on TV I want to watch," Cassidy said sheepishly.

"So tape it," Melanie said. "Don't you have a VCR?"

Cassidy shook her head. "I want to watch it live." She gave Rebound a last swipe with the sweat scraper and turned him around to lead him out of the washrack. "Thanks for the invitation though. You guys have a great time," she said cheerfully. She started to lead Rebound back toward the barn, hoping to escape without having to explain any further.

Dylan stepped in front of her, blocking the way. "Hey, it's not like you to be so secretive," he said gently. "What's up?"

Cassidy paused. Then she sighed. She guessed she'd have to tell them—there didn't seem to be any way around it. She hoped they would understand. Because when she told them about the horse, she'd have to tell them about her father. "It's a . . . a horse race," Cassidy finally said.

3

"A HORSE RACE?" CHRISTINA ASKED INCREDULOUSLY. "Since when are you into racing?"

"What race is today?" Melanie said, thinking aloud. "Oh, I know! The Ruffian Handicap, right?" She frowned. "Why are you so interested in that?"

"Because Lady T is running," Cassidy told them.

"Who's Lady T?" Dylan asked.

"Dylan! Everybody knows who Lady T is," Melanie exclaimed.

"Well, I don't," Dylan said. "Who is she?"

"She's one of the greatest race horses in the country," Christina said.

"In the world," Melanie corrected her.

Cassidy smiled. "It's true that she's one of the best. She won the Filly Triple Crown this year."

"She set track records all over the country. And not

26

just for fillies," Melanie offered. "She's beating the boys."

"She's not as fast as Pizzazz," Christina argued.

"Yes, she is. She'd beat Pizzazz if she ever ran against him," Melanie said.

"Who's Pizzazz?" Dylan asked.

"Dylan!" Melanie said in disbelief. "Pizzazz is the horse that won the Kentucky Derby this year. And the Preakness," Cassidy told him. "Then he stumbled coming out of the gate in the Belmont Stakes and was beaten by a nose. Everyone thought he was going to win the Triple Crown."

"He would have, if he hadn't stumbled," Christina said.

"I can't believe you don't know who Pizzazz is," Melanie said to Dylan.

"Okay, Miss Know-it-all, who's Jordi Santos?" Dylan countered.

"Never heard of him," Melanie said.

"I know," Cassidy said. "He's a soccer player. For a California team, I think."

"Right," Dylan said. "He's one of the top goalies in the country. Probably in the world. Melanie!" he exclaimed, mimicking Melanie's tone of voice. "I can't believe you didn't know that."

"Well, I don't keep up with soccer," Melanie said.

"I don't keep up with racing," Dylan retorted.

"Anyway, why's this such an important race?" Christina asked Cassidy.

"I'm just . . . really interested in the horse," Cassidy said. *I may as well go on and tell them*, she thought. "My dad is Lady T's owner." She delivered this information and watched the other kids expectantly, to see how they would react.

"No way!" Melanie said. "Really?"

"Your Dad owns Lady T?" Christina asked.

Cassidy nodded. "He . . . used to be involved in racing, when we lived in Miami," Cassidy said carefully.

"Involved how?" Christina asked.

"He was a trainer," Cassidy said.

"Really," Christina mused. "Did he train any big-name horses?"

"Sure," Cassidy said. "Lots. He was one of the biggest trainers in Florida."

"What are the names of some of them?" Christina asked.

Christina sounded skeptical. Even Dylan was giving her a disbelieving look. "Ever hear of a horse called Battenburg?" Cassidy asked.

"Sure," Christina said. "He won the Derby a couple of years ago."

"He's a famous stud horse now," Melanie added.

"Right," Cassidy said. "My dad trained him." She thought Christina still looked skeptical look so she went on. "And he trained Sidewinder, and Windsong, and Bucket O' Rocks. And Surfer Girl," she added, thinking of one more.

"Your dad trained all those horses?" Melanie asked.

"Yep," Cassidy said.

"I've heard of some of them," Melanie said. "Bucket O' Rocks just won a big stakes race, didn't he?"

"That's right," Cassidy said.

"Oh, sure, even I've heard of him," Dylan joked.

"Trib, stop it," Melanie said, interrupting the horse talk. Cassidy saw that Trib was bulldozing toward a patch of particularly lush grass, dragging Melanie along with him.

"Get his head up, Melanie," Christina ordered. "And pay attention will you? He'll drag you all the way home if you don't watch what you're doing."

"Speaking of which, it's about time we got going, don't you think?" Melanie said, lugging Trib's head up.

Cassidy glanced at the sky, which was growing paler as the afternoon faded into evening. Rebound's shadow, and her own beside him, were stretched long by the slanting rays of the low sun. She judged that it must be nearly six o'clock. The race started at seven. "I've got to get going," she said.

"Hey, I have an idea," Dylan said. "Why don't we all watch the race together?"

"That's a great idea," Katie said.

"Why don't we all go to our house," Melanie suggested.

"Yeah, you guys have the killer TV," Dylan said enthusiastically. "I'm there." He turned to Cassidy. "What about you, Cass? Want to watch it at Christina's house? They have this giant screen TV. It's so cool."

Cassidy glanced at Christina. "Am I invited?" she asked politely.

"Of course you're invited," Melanie said impatiently.

"We'll have to check with Mom first," Christina reminded her cousin.

"She's not going to care. Here," Melanie said, holding Trib's reins out to Christina. "If you hold him for a minute, I'll call her."

"No way," Christina said. "Sterling won't like him so close to her."

"I'll hold him," Cassidy said. "Rebound won't mind." She took the double-set of Trib's reins in one hand, while she continued to hold Rebound's reins in the other. Trib kept trying to reach down to graze, but Cassidy wouldn't let him. She didn't want him dragging her around while she was trying to hold both horses. She was thinking that maybe it would be fun to watch the race at Christina's house. And it would be cool to see it on a big screen TV—almost like being there.

Melanie was back in two minutes. She wore a serious, sorrowful expression. "She . . . she said 'no,'" Melanie told them in a stricken voice.

"Why?" Christina asked, sounding shocked.

Melanie gazed at them all, her brown eyes looking sadder than ever. Then suddenly, she grinned. "Just kidding!" she chirped. "She said it was fine."

"Melanie!" Christina picked up a handful of grass and threw it at her.

Melanie easily dodged the small shower of green blades. "Hah! Fooled you, didn't I?"

Christina rolled her eyes. "You are so weird," she said.

"Come on, let's get going," Melanie said, leading Trib over to his saddle, which was propped against the side of the barn.

"We'll meet you at Whitebrook as soon as we call our parents," Katie said.

"Okay, see you in a few," Christina said. She and Melanie tacked up their horses and mounted up.

Cassidy watched the girls ride toward the gate that separated Mona's pasture from the back acres of Whitebrook Farm. Then she led Rebound into the barn and put him away in his stall. "G'night, Rebound," she said fondly, giving him a quick kiss on the nose.

Cassidy slipped off Rebound's blue nylon halter and hung it on the hook outside his stall door. Then she slid the door closed and went to take a quick peak at her other horse.

Wellington, Cassidy's four-year-old Thoroughbred hunter, was in the stall next door, peacefully munching his hay. When he heard the latch on his door click open, he swung his head around expectantly. "Hi, Welly," Cassidy said, sliding the door open just wide enough to peep through.

Wellington, who was always talkative, greeted Cassidy with a low whinny. She smiled with pleasure. "I'm glad to see you, too," she said. Then, unable to resist, she slid the door open wider and slipped through. "How's my handsome boy?" she murmured, sliding her hand down the length of his slender neck over and over again. Wellington's chestnut coat was cool and soft under her hand. She marveled at how silky he felt compared to Rebound's thicker, fuzzier coat. Down in Miami, where it was always warm, Welly's coat stayed soft and sleek. She wondered if he would grow a winter coat now that they were in a cooler climate. She leaned against his shoulder. "What would I ever do without you and Rebound?" she said softly.

The move to Kentucky that spring had been a sudden one. When she thought of the circumstances surrounding the move, Cassidy still felt dazed. One day she'd been happily schooling her horses at the stable where she'd ridden for years. The next, she'd found herself in her bedroom, packing her belongings in boxes, trying to make sense of the intense bits of dialogue she overheard from her parents down the hall.

"But, Harrison, how could they blame you?" her mother had said.

"Because I was in charge," her father had replied in a grim voice.

"But if they told you to . . . I don't see how they can just take away—"

"Ssh! I don't want the kids to . . ."

They had lowered their voices again. Cassidy strained to hear, but the most she could make out was that something had happened at the track where her father was a trainer, and it was something so bad that they had to leave Miami. It wasn't until days later that she had managed to piece together the whole story, not from the cryptic explanation her parents gave her, but from a newspaper article her brother Campbell had shown her.

"Take a look at this," he'd said, handing Cassidy the paper. The headline had shocked her. It read, to her horror, FLORIDA OWNERS AND TRAINERS SUSPECTED IN DEATHS OF THREE HORSES.

Just then, there was the first rattle of feed being dropped into a horse's manger, and instantly all the horses in the barn began clamoring for their dinner with urgent stomps and whinnies. Wellington gave a hungry nicker and pointed his ears toward the sound of the feed cart.

Cassidy glanced up and saw Dylan peering at her through the open stall door. "Hey, Cassidy, my mom's here," he said. "Do you want to ride with me over to Christina's?"

"Oh. Yeah, sure." Cassidy said, trying to sound cheerful. "Bye, Welly," she said, giving the horse a last pat. He barely paid any attention to her, he was so intent on his approaching dinner.

"Did you call your Mom?" Dylan asked as she slid the stall door closed.

"She's not home," Cassidy explained. "I just have to call my brother and tell him not to pick me up—um—

that is, if your Mom doesn't mind giving me a ride home later, too."

"No problem," Dylan said. "Katie's coming, too."

Cassidy used the phone in the barn office to call home. Then she climbed into one of the middle seats of the Beckers' minivan, next to Katie.

"Hi, Cassidy!" Dylan's little sisters waved happily at her from the seat behind hers.

"Hi, Violet. Hi, Madeleine," Cassidy said, smiling at the nine-year-old and the two-year-old. Both girls showed matching, dimpled grins. "They are so cute," Cassidy said to Dylan. "Maybe I could baby-sit for them sometime."

"Sure, you can have my job anytime," Dylan said emphatically.

"Yeah, Mommy, we want Cassidy to baby-sit us! Not Dylan," Violet said, sticking out her tongue at her brother.

"We want Cassidy!" Madeleine agreed.

"I'll keep it in mind," said Sarah Becker, Dylan's mom.

"Can she baby-sit us tonight?" Violet asked.

"She's busy, dear, and tonight your father and I aren't going out."

In just a few minutes, the tires of the van were crunching on the white gravel driveway of Whitebrook Farm. Cassidy had only been there once before. She found herself leaning forward for a better view of the place. There were white-fenced paddocks on either side of the drive where sleek mares, colts, and fillies were turned out. Beyond the paddocks were the barns: three long, red buildings arranged in a U shape. Nearby were several matching outbuildings and more paddocks.

Christina's house was a big, white, two-story wood-frame farmhouse, its shutters painted brick-red to match the barns. Cassidy wondered which of the lace-curtained windows on the second floor were Christina's. She tried to imagine what Christina's room would look like, but what came to mind instead was her old bedroom in the house in Miami, with its polished-wood floors and its tall windows shaded by giant live-oaks dripping with Spanish moss. She missed it terribly.

The Smiths were renting a plain brick house in a subdivision just outside of town. The rooms were small, with high, aluminum-framed windows, and an ugly green carpet covered all the floors. Cassidy hated the new house. Most of her things were still packed in boxes stacked in the carport, because she hadn't had the heart to unpack them. Her parents kept saying cheerfully it was only temporary, that soon they'd buy a bigger house, and that the move had been so sudden they just hadn't had time to look for a nicer place. But it had been months now since they'd left Miami. Cassidy had begun to worry that her parents weren't really going to buy another house. Nobody had actually told her anything, but more than once she had heard her parents arguing about money after she and Campbell had gone to bed.

"Cassidy?"

Dylan was looking at her strangely. For a second, Cassidy had the odd feeling that he had somehow read her thoughts. She felt her cheeks turn bright red.

"What?" she asked.

"Do you want to open the door?"

"Oh!" Cassidy laughed, still feeling embarrassed. "Sorry."

Violet was giggling at her. "And just what's so funny, miss?" Cassidy said, pretending to scowl at her. Then she smiled and ruffled Violet's hair playfully. "See you soon. Bye, Madeleine," she said, and slid the big side door of the van open.

Cassidy could see another house across from the barns, a two-story stone cottage with the same matching red shutters. She wondered who lived there. Just beyond the cottage she glimpsed a section of the training track, with its inner turf course and the blue metal starting gate standing empty. The barns and buildings around her looked nothing like the ones at the track in Miami where her father had worked, but the place reminded Cassidy of it just the same. There was the same feel in the air that all busy farms had at the end of the day—the few hours of peace when the work was done, the waiting time before it started all over again: the stalls to be mucked, the buckets filled, the horses groomed and exercised and bathed and brushed, the clanging of the gate, the swish of a broom on the floor, the rustle of hay being tossed into stalls, and most of all the sounds and smells of horses at work. The quiet was loaded with the promise of the business of running a racing stable, and Cassidy missed it keenly.

All summer she had tried hard not to let her family's situation get to her. She had practically lived at Mona's farm, because when she was jumping Rebound in the outdoor ring or hacking Wellington on the cross-country trails, she could forget about what had happened in Miami and just feel happy for a while. She had made friends with the other kids as well as she could, without telling them much about her past. As long as she had her horses, she thought she would make it all right.

Somewhere deep in her heart Cassidy had thought that, after a while, everything would work out just fine, and living in Kentucky would be just as good as living in Miami had ever been. But seeing Whitebrook Farm, it suddenly became clear to Cassidy just how much her life had changed. Tears welled at the backs of her eyes, and she had to bite her lip hard as she realized that, no matter what she wished or how hard she tried to ignore it, nothing was ever going to be quite the same.

4

"HI, GUYS." MELANIE WAS COMING OUT OF ONE OF THE barns, waving extravagantly at them. She hiked up the path and joined them in the parking area.

Cassidy quickly wiped her hand across her eyes and took a deep breath, hoping no one would notice that she had been crying.

"Where's Christina?" Katie asked.

"Oh, you know, kissing Sterling goodnight for the eight hundred millionth time. She'll be joining us sometime next year," Melanie said, starting for the house. "Come on, let's go inside. We can order a pizza before the race starts."

They followed Melanie down the path that led to the picket-fenced backyard. They left their shoes in the mud room by the back door and went through the big farmhouse kitchen into the den. Melanie picked

38

up the phone and called the pizza place.

"Isn't that the biggest television you've ever seen?" Dylan said, plopping down on the fluffy, overstuffed couch.

"It is," Cassidy agreed. She looked around, trying to decide where to sit. Melanie had commandeered the big leather armchair, and Katie had taken the old wooden rocker. That left the couch. She sat down at the opposite end from Dylan.

"Aunt Ashleigh hates it, but Uncle Mike says he got it because when he can't be at a race, the big screen is just as good," Melanie said, peeling off her socks. "But I think that's just an excuse. He really just likes to watch football games on it!"

"So? What's wrong with that?" Dylan demanded.

"Aunt Ashleigh hates what?"

Cassidy looked up to see who had spoken. Ashleigh Griffen stood in the doorway, surveying them calmly. As always, Cassidy thought that Ashleigh looked more like Christina's sister than her mother. If there was any gray in her dark, curly hair, Cassidy couldn't see it, and Ashleigh's hazel eyes sparkled with energy. Years of riding and working with horses had kept her fit and muscular. She was slim and small, jockey-sized; Cassidy knew if she stood up she would easily be several inches taller than Ashleigh.

"Aunt Ashleigh hates what?" Ashleigh repeated.

"Oh, we were talking about Uncle Mike getting the big-screen TV," Melanie explained.

"You're right, I do hate it," Ashleigh agreed. "But your uncle couldn't live without it."

There was the bang of a screen door in the background and Christina appeared in the kitchen behind her mom. "Hi," she said.

Christina was half a head taller than Ashleigh. Her strawberry-blond hair was still dark and damp with sweat from her riding helmet and a sprinkle of freckles showed across the bridge of her nose. Cassidy could see that Christina resembled both of her parents. She was tall and lanky like her father, but her coloring was like her mother's. Her hair wasn't as dark, but Christina's hazel eyes were exactly like Ashleigh's.

"Is the race starting?" Christina asked.

Cassidy glanced at her watch, then at the television, which was already showing some of the pre-race rituals. Statistics on the Ruffian Handicap from last year were listed on the screen. "It should be starting in about ten minutes," Cassidy said. She kept glancing at the screen, hoping for a shot of Lady T.

"Did we order a pizza?" Christina asked.

"Yep," Melanie said. "Should be here any minute."

"Good. I'm starving." Christina went over and plopped down on the couch between Dylan and Cassidy.

"Where's Kevin?" Ashleigh asked. "Why don't you invite him over for pizza, too? I know Beth is working tonight."

"I'll call him," Melanie chirped.

Cassidy saw Christina and Dylan exchange meaningful looks, but she wasn't sure what it meant. A few minutes later though, when Kevin bounded through the kitchen and into the den, she thought she understood. Melanie's whole face lit up when Kevin came in; obviously she had a big crush on him.

"Hi, guys," Kevin said, plunking himself down on the hassock at the foot of Melanie's chair. He had wavy auburn hair and green eyes, and a generous sprinkle of freckles showed through his end-of-summer tan. Cassidy had met Kevin early in the summer; he and Dylan played on the same baseball team, and Cassidy had been to some of the games.

They all said hello. "How'd you get here so fast?" Cassidy asked curiously.

Kevin gave her a strange look. "I live right next door," he said, pointing out the big picture window overlooking the acres of fenced pasture.

Puzzled, Cassidy looked out the window. "Next door?"

"In the cottage. My dad's Ian McLean, the head trainer here," Kevin explained.

"Oh!" Cassidy remembered the stone cottage she'd seen on her way in. "So, have you lived here long?"

Kevin nodded. "All my life."

"Unfortunately for the rest of us," Christina teased him.

"You're lucky," Cassidy said wistfully.

"So where's the 'za?" Kevin asked, looking around.

41

"I'm starving! Melanie," he said, poking her playfully. "You promised to feed me, remember? Come on, girl, get in the kitchen and start cooking!"

"You don't want anything she cooks, believe me," Christina said.

"Oh, I forgot. The only thing Melanie knows how to fix is Kool-aid," Kevin teased. He was referring to Melanie's hair, which was very blond, except where she had streaked it orange and red with Kool-aid.

Melanie responded by shoving Kevin off the hassock with one foot. Kevin, not to be outdone, grabbed her by the ankle and pulled her off the chair onto the floor. The wrestling match was interrupted by the arrival of the pizza, and by the time they had each loaded up a paper plate, it was time for the race to start.

Melanie turned up the volume on the television so they could hear the commentary on the horses as they paraded down the track to the post.

"Now, what race is this?" Kevin asked.

"It's the Ruffian Handicap," Melanie told him. "It's a Grade I handicap race for fillies and mares."

"Who's that horse?" Kevin said excitedly.

Melanie snapped her head around to look at the television screen and Kevin took the opportunity to steal a couple of mushrooms off Melanie's pizza. When she turned around, he was chewing placidly, with a completely straight face. Cassidy and Katie stifled giggles, and Christina snorted around a bite of pizza, which made everyone laugh even harder.

"What's so funny?" Melanie asked.

"Nothing," Kevin said innocently. "Look, isn't that Ruffian?" he said, pointing suddenly at the television.

"It can't be," Melanie said as she turned to look, and again Kevin snatched a couple of mushrooms. "Ruffian's—hey!" Melanie's pizza was now looking conspicuously bare. She eyed the others suspiciously. "Okay, who's been taking my mushrooms?" Her gaze came to rest on Kevin, who was just stuffing a last bite of mushroom-loaded pizza into his mouth. "Kevin!" Melanie said indignantly.

"What?" Kevin looked off toward the ceiling, chewing innocently.

"Quit stealing my mushrooms!" Melanie warned him. "Or I'll handicap you."

"Who's Ruffian?" Dylan asked.

"She was a racehorse," Christina told him. "One of the greatest ever. She won every race she ever ran."

"And she set records at racetracks all over the country," Melanie added.

"Didn't she break her leg or something, in some big race?" Katie asked.

Melanie nodded. "It was so sad. She was beating the other horse, and then all of a sudden, crack, her leg just snapped. And do you know what? She kept on trying to run. The jockey was doing his best to stop her but she kept on galloping, even though her leg was useless."

"That's so sad," Katie said.

"She had heart," Cassidy said, thinking of Mona's

words to them earlier. She kept her eye on the screen, waiting for a glimpse of Lady T.

"How come there were only two horses in the race?" Dylan asked.

"It was a match race," Melanie explained. "Between Ruffian and. . . oh, who was that other horse?"

"Foolish Pleasure," Ashleigh volunteered. "He was the favorite colt that year. He'd won the Derby and was cleaning up in races everywhere. Ruffian had won the Filly Triple Crown, and the public wanted to see the greatest colt in the country run against the greatest filly ever."

"Wow, wouldn't it be cool if they did that with Lady T and Pizzazz?"

"What, you mean have a match race between them?" Ashleigh frowned. "I doubt that would happen. They're both great horses, but they're from opposite sides of the country. Lady T trains in Florida and Pizzazz in California. The logistics of staging a race like that are so complicated. Where would they race?"

"Look, there she is!" Cassidy said excitedly, pointing to the screen. There was a close-up shot of a Thoroughbred filly being ponied to the gate by a man on a buckskin.

"There who is?" Dylan asked.

"Lady T," Cassidy said. Then the terrible homesick feeling came back, twisting in her stomach so that she had to put down her pizza. She stared at the bay filly trotting down the track and felt farther away from

44

home than ever. How could her whole life have changed so much in such a short time?

"Look, they're loading Lady T," Melanie said.

They watched Lady T as the assistant starters loaded her into the gate. The filly walked gracefully into the metal enclosure, just as calmly as if she were entering her own stall. Two more horses were loaded into the sixth and seventh positions. The number eight horse, a big chestnut filly, trotted up to the gate, then at the last second stopped and began backing up. She fought her handlers, tossing her head in defiance. Then she reared, but somehow the jockey stayed on, and when she put her front feet down, the assistant starters were able to lead her right into the gate.

"Wow, that one sure didn't want to go in," Dylan remarked.

"Some of them just have to show off a little before they go in the gate," Melanie said. "I've noticed that from working around them so much. They cut up and play a little, but then when they've had enough they just go, 'Okay, time to go to work,' and they get right down to business. There's this one horse we have right now, Saturday Affair, that—"

"Melanie, shush," Christina said. "They're about to start."

At that moment they shut the gate behind the last horse and the bell sounded the start of the race.

"There they go!" Cassidy exclaimed.

For a few seconds everyone was silent, watching the

pack of ten mares and fillies as they exploded from the gate and tore down the dirt track. By the time they had gone an eighth of a mile, the group had spread out more, with the feisty number-eight horse in the lead on the inside and Lady T behind her by half a length. The track was sloppy from a spring shower earlier in the day, and on the big television screen Cassidy could see the mud splattering in the faces of the horses and jockeys.

". . . and it's That's My Girl in front, with the favorite Lady T second, followed by Thumbelina and Star Cat . . ." the announcer droned.

Cassidy felt her heart thudding in her chest. She'd been around horses and racetracks all her life, but somehow it was different watching Lady T run. The little bay filly seemed to represent all that was left of Cassidy's old, familiar life, and suddenly Cassidy felt as if she were out there running with Lady T. "Go, go, go," she found herself whispering as the horses rounded the first turn of the mile and one-sixteenth race.

Lady T had been nosing up on the lead horse, slowly but surely. Now they were neck and neck. Suddenly the horse in front began to pull away. A length, then two, and they were rounding the second turn. A horse from near the back of the pack began moving up on the outside, passing other horses, but clearly the race was between Lady T and That's My Girl.

"And That's My Girl is making a run for it, pulling away from Lady T," the announcer said.

"No way!" Melanie said, jumping to her feet. "Come on, Lady T! You can't let that no-class horse beat you!"

The horses were coming down the stretch to the wire, and Lady T was still a length behind That's My Girl. "Come on, Lady T," Cassidy said fiercely, crossing the fingers on both her hands. With all her might she willed Lady T to pull ahead of the other horse.

And then, as if she had heard, Lady T suddenly bounded forward, the length of her stride seeming to double, as if That's My Girl was running in slow motion next to her. In half a second Lady T had passed her and then opened up her lead by a length, then two, then three. It was as if she'd been playing with the other horse, just trying to see what she had in her. At the wire, Lady T was ahead by five lengths, and That's My Girl had burned out, dropping back to fourth behind Star Cat and a filly called Miss Pandora.

"That's My Girl fades in the home stretch, and Lady T runs away with the Ruffian Handicap!"

"Whoo-hoo!" Melanie cheered.

"All right!" Cassidy said happily. She was panting as if she had been riding in the race herself, and she realized she must have been holding her breath.

"That was a pretty exciting race," Dylan admitted.

"Yeah, I like it when you don't know who's going to win until the last second," Kevin agreed.

"What do you mean? There was never any doubt who was going to win," Cassidy said. "It was Lady T all the way."

"Hey, that should be great for your dad, right?" Christina said.

Cassidy nodded. Lady T's win would definitely make some money for her dad.

"What's that?" Ashleigh still stood in the doorway where she had been watching the race, arms folded, looking keenly at Cassidy. "Your father owns that horse?"

"Yes," Cassidy said. She tried to keep her voice calm, but she was proud. She glanced at the screen, where reporters were interviewing the jockey who had ridden Lady T.

"Who's your dad?" Ashleigh asked curiously.

Cassidy hesitated. She hadn't wanted anyone to know about her father. She was pretty sure the kids wouldn't have heard about what had happened in Miami, but Ashleigh was in the horse business; she would know all about it. And like everyone else, Cassidy reflected, Ashleigh would probably think that Cassidy's father had been responsible for the deaths of those horses back home. But there was no way to cover it up. *Oh, boy,* she thought. *Here it comes.*

She gazed directly into Ashleigh's dark eyes, expecting the usual look of disapproval. "My father is Harrison Smith," Cassidy said.

5

"HARRISON SMITH!" ASHLEIGH EXCLAIMED. "REALLY?" To Cassidy's surprise, a broad smile broke over Ashleigh's face.

"Do you—do you know my dad?" Cassidy asked.

"I sure do," Ashleigh said.

Cassidy gave Ashleigh a curious look. "How do you know him?" she asked.

"I met your dad down in Florida, years ago," Ashleigh said. "We had taken some horses down to Gulfstream Park, and your dad had some horses there, too. That was back in the days when I was still in business with Clay Townsend and his son, Brad." She made a face, as if she were tasting something bad. "Anyway, we got all the way down there, and they claimed they didn't have stalls for us. Brad had been in charge of making the arrangements, and he'd only reserved

49

space for his two horses. So there I was, with four horses that had just been shipped a thousand miles, all ready to race and with no place to stay."

"Oh, poor Mom," Christina said. "What'd you do?"

"This was way back in my early days of running a stable," Ashleigh went on. "It was the first time Mr. Townsend, Brad's father, had put me completely in charge and I was about to fail miserably."

"Did you call Uncle Mike?" Melanie asked.

Ashleigh shook her head. "Mike was back in Kentucky running his dad's farm. There was nothing he could do."

"So what'd you do?" Kevin asked.

"Well, Brad was absolutely no help. He unloaded his two horses and left me to fend for myself. And I was determined not to bother Mr. Townsend. I was sure if I didn't handle the situation myself, he would never send me out again," Ashleigh said. "But I was completely at a loss. I couldn't think of anything to do, except turn around and drive back to Townsend Acres. I was sitting on the running board of the truck, working up a good cry, when I noticed a pair of blue cowboy boots walk up and stop in front of me."

Cassidy smiled. "Dad," she said, thinking fondly of him. Her dad owned a pair of battered leather cowboy boots that had once been a startlingly bright shade of blue.

"That's right," Ashleigh agreed. "Your dad introduced himself to me and asked why I looked so upset. I told him I had a trailer full of horses that were supposed to run and no place to unload them, and he told me he had a couple of stalls at his place, and I was welcome to board them there if I liked.

"'Where's your place?' I asked him, and he pointed at a good-sized barn not fifty feet away."

Cassidy nodded. "He kept an aisle in one of the barns at Gulfstream Park. It was where he first started working as a trainer." She risked a glance around at the other kids and noticed with relief that they were all listening to the story with interest. Nobody seemed to be disapproving, least of all Ashleigh.

"Harrison saved my life that day," Ashleigh said with real appreciation in her voice. "At least, it seemed like it to me at the time. He let me keep my horses in his aisle for the two weeks we were supposed to be down there, and he didn't even charge me. He also gave me some valuable training tips. And he was a super-nice guy. We got to be pretty good friends while I was there, but we never really kept in touch." Ashleigh smiled warmly at Cassidy. "I had no idea you were Harrison Smith's daughter. It would be great to see him. How is your dad?"

"He's . . . fine," Cassidy said. In fact, she was worried about her father. He had acted cheerful about the move, refusing to let the terrible accusations against him get him down. But Cassidy could tell he was stressed. And no matter how cheerful he pretended to be, nothing could hide the fact that her father was miserable when he wasn't around horses.

"That was such a shame that he was caught in the middle of that insurance fraud scandal, with those horses in Miami," Ashleigh said softly.

"Insurance fraud?" Christina asked.

"What kind of insurance fraud? What horses?" Melanie wanted to know.

Cassidy cringed. She had been hoping Ashleigh wouldn't bring it up.

"There was a fire in one of the barns at Calder, the racetrack in Miami," Ashleigh said. "Three horses were killed."

"Oh, no, that's terrible," Katie said.

"It is," Ashleigh said. "But the odd thing was, it wasn't a big fire. Someone saw the smoke before it got out of hand and they put it out quickly. There was hardly even any damage. And although there were lots of horses stabled there, only those three horses died, apparently from smoke inhalation. Their stalls were all in the same end of the barn."

"Do you think somebody set the fire on purpose?" Dylan asked.

"Somebody definitely set the fire on purpose," Ashleigh said. "The investigation showed that right away."

"So what did Cassidy's dad have to do with it?" Kevin asked.

"My dad was training those horses," Cassidy said. "Everybody blamed the fire on my dad."

"Did your dad do it?" Melanie asked solemnly.

"Of course not!" Cassidy said sharply. "My father loves horses. He would never ever do something like that!"

"Well, why were they trying to blame it on him?" Melanie asked.

"Dad had been having some problems with the owners. They wanted him to use this drug on their horses that was supposed to make them perform better," Cassidy said.

"But that's illegal!" Melanie protested.

"I know," Cassidy said.

"Cassidy's dad was in a sticky position," Ashleigh interjected. "When you're a trainer, you depend on the horse owners to pay you for training your horses. And you get a percentage of the winnings from races won by the horses you train. Some owners really put their trust in the trainer. But others try to have a say in everything that happens to their horse. If they want the trainer to do something, and the trainer doesn't agree with them, they might just move the horse to another trainer," she explained.

"So if your dad didn't do what the owners wanted, he would lose those clients?" Katie asked.

Cassidy nodded.

"So, what did he do?" Christina asked. "Give them the drugs?"

"No, he wouldn't," Cassidy said. "But that same week, two of the horses won races, and they both tested positive for drugs."

"But I thought you said your dad wouldn't do it," Dylan protested.

"He didn't," Cassidy said. "Dad told the stewards he didn't have anything to do with it, but the owners said he must have. They all got fined. Then there was the fire."

"But who set the fire?" Melanie wanted to know.

"It sounds like the owners did it, doesn't it? But why would they?" Christina mused. "You can't win races without horses."

"I don't know," Cassidy said sadly. "I just know it ruined everything."

"I know," Kevin said. "I bet they did it for the insurance money."

"That's what it looked like," Ashleigh said. "It just so happened that these horses were all insured for a lot of money. The owners tried to say that Cassidy's dad was responsible for the fire—that he had set it because he was angry that the owners had threatened to find another trainer for their horses."

"That's terrible," Katie said. "Did they ever prove who really set the fire?"

"Unfortunately not," Ashleigh said.

"My dad was at another racetrack a hundred miles away when the fire happened," Cassidy added.

"So how come he got blamed for the deaths of the horses?" Dylan asked.

"Remember I told you that the fire wasn't really that big?" Ashleigh said. "They discovered that the horses

54

hadn't died from smoke inhalation after all. The autopsies showed that the horses had traces of poison in their systems."

"Poison!" Katie exclaimed. "Who would have done that?"

"Well, apparently whoever poisoned them set the fire to make it look like the horses died from the smoke," Ashleigh said.

"Those poor horses," Katie said.

Cassidy nodded. She couldn't bring herself to say that Lady T had been in the same barn when the fire happened. That the beautiful, talented filly might have lost her life in that senseless fire filled her with anger. Cassidy realized she was clenching her fists, and she made herself uncurl them.

"They couldn't prove that Harrison did it," Ashleigh went on, "but because he was the trainer in charge, his license was suspended."

"That doesn't seem fair," Melanie said. "If they couldn't prove he had done anything wrong, how could they take away his trainer's license?"

"That's what we all thought," Cassidy said. "Luckily it was only a six-month suspension. Dad said they went easy on him."

"Easy!" Kevin exclaimed. "He can't work for six months even though nobody can prove he killed the horses? That seems pretty harsh if you ask me."

"I know," Cassidy said. "But Dad explained it to me. The rules are there to protect everybody: the trainers, the owners, the jockeys, and most of all the horses. Somebody has to be held accountable when a horse is hurt, because the horse can't tell who did it. Dad was the trainer in charge, so Dad had to pay. He says somebody had to be punished for the crime, to keep other dishonest people from trying the same thing."

"I understand," Kevin said. "But it seems so unfair to your dad."

Cassidy shrugged. "They could have suspended him for years, or even for life. But even if he hadn't been suspended at all, Dad couldn't work in Florida anymore. He said no one would want him to train their horses after he was connected with a scandal like that."

Cassidy searched the faces of the other kids, trying to read their thoughts. *Did they think, like most people, that her father probably* had *killed those horses?*

Dylan was looking sideways at Cassidy. "Is that why your family moved to Kentucky?" he asked gently.

Cassidy nodded. Suddenly it was difficult to speak.

"Didn't they get the owners in trouble, too?" Kevin asked.

Cassidy shook her head. "But I don't think they got the insurance money," she managed to say.

"I hope they never do," Christina said. "But how did your dad end up owning Lady T?"

Cassidy smiled, thinking of the gorgeous little filly who had just won the Ruffian Handicap. "Lady T was his big investment. He got her as a yearling, at a bank-

56

ruptcy auction. She didn't do much in her two-year-old year, but this year she's been doing great!" Cassidy said proudly.

"She sure has," Ashleigh agreed.

"It's about the only good thing that's happened to my dad this year," Cassidy said sadly. "Poor Dad. He hates his new job."

"I bet," Ashleigh said. "When I knew your father he was so passionate about the horse business. After spending so many years around horses it must be really hard for him to be away from them."

Cassidy nodded. "It's a good thing he was able to keep Lady T," she said softly. "She's the only thing he has left."

"Can't he train horses here in Kentucky?" Christina asked.

"Not until his suspension is lifted," Ashleigh said. "The Racing Commission in each state has what's known as reciprocity. That means that if a trainer is suspended in one state, it goes for all of them."

"He only has one more month to go though. Then he can go back to work as a trainer—if anyone here will hire him." Cassidy sighed. "I wish there was some way to just erase all the bad stuff that happened in Miami," she said.

Melanie said, "Hey, how much money does your dad get from the race?"

"Huh?" Cassidy answered.

"You know, the race. The Ruffian Handicap. The

purse was twenty thousand dollars. How much does your dad get?" Melanie demanded.

Cassidy had forgotten about the prize money. For a second it cheered her. She thought for a moment. "Well, he has to pay someone else to train her now that he can't do it. And that's pretty expensive. Plus her board and all the other bills . . . I don't know, maybe five thousand dollars?" she guessed.

"That's all?" Melanie said skeptically.

Cassidy nodded gloomily.

The phone rang. "I got it," Christina said, leaping off the couch to answer it. "Hi, Dad," she said into the phone. "Sure, she's right here. It's Dad," she said, handing the phone to Ashleigh.

"Mike?" Ashleigh said. "What's up?" She listened intently for a moment. "Really . . . Well, what did you tell them? Uh-huh. Hang on, I'll be right down." Ashleigh hung up the phone. "I have to run down to the barn office," she said. "Something's come up."

Cassidy didn't know Ashleigh well enough to guess what was going on, but she could tell from the change in her manner that it must be something important. She was curious, but not quite bold enough to ask what it might be.

The screen door banged shut behind Ashleigh. "What do you think is going on?" Melanie asked Christina.

"Who knows?" Christina said with a shrug. "With horses, it's always something."

"Well, I guess I'd better call my mom," Dylan said. "Chris, can I use the phone?"

"Sure," Christina said. "Here." She tossed him the cordless phone.

"Katie, do you need a ride?" he asked, punching in the numbers.

"Yeah, if your mom doesn't mind," Katie said.

"And you, too, right, Cassidy?" Dylan asked.

"Oh . . . um, yes, please," Cassidy said, feeling even more downcast. The thought of going home made her feel discouraged. She dreaded seeing the worn looks of tension on her parents' faces. Most of all, she was sick of worrying. All day she had tried to forget about the terrible thing she'd heard her parents say. During the lesson with Mona, it had been easy to forget it all and just concentrate on riding. Then it had been time for the race, so she had tried just to be excited about Lady T. But now that it was time to go home, there was no way to avoid it any longer. Cassidy stared at the braided rug on the Reeses' living room floor, willing herself not to cry. But the tears came anyway, burning the back of her throat and glazing her eyes so that the rug dissolved into a jumble of colored blotches.

"Mom? Can you come get us now?" Dylan was saying. Cassidy heard him put the phone down. Then he must have noticed her. "Cassidy? What's wrong?" he asked.

"Are you crying?" Melanie asked, her voice suddenly and uncharacteristically soft.

Cassidy knew everyone must be looking at her. She looked up at them, willing herself not to blink.

"Cassidy, are you okay? What's the matter?" Katie asked.

Could she say it? Cassidy wondered. Saying it might help. On the other hand, if she didn't say it, it might not happen. Talking about things, she knew, could sometimes make them real.

"Did something happen?" Kevin asked.

They were all looking at her. Cassidy's throat ached so much that she didn't know how she could speak, even if she wanted to. "I . . . my . . ." she tried.

"What?" Dylan asked.

"My dad . . ." Cassidy managed to say. She tried to keep her chin from trembling, tried to keep her face relaxed. The tears began to spill down her cheeks. "Last night I heard my parents talking. They said . . ." She struggled to keep her voice from breaking. "They said they might have to sell Lady T!" she blurted out, sobbing.

6

EVERYONE WAS STUNNED. NOBODY SPOKE. CASSIDY SAT ON the couch and cried miserably. *Stupid,* she thought. *What did I tell them that for?* She put a hand across her eyes, struggling to get control of herself. She knew her face was bright red, both from the tears and from embarrassment.

Melanie finally spoke. "But, why?" she asked.

Cassidy swiped furiously at her eyes and sniffed. "Because they need the money," she said. "They're having really bad financial problems and they can't afford to keep her anymore." There. She had said it. Now they knew everything about her. She took a deep breath, feeling completely humiliated.

"Wow. That is seriously bad news," Kevin said.

"Do they really have to sell her?" Melanie asked.

"Isn't there anything else they can do?" Christina asked, sounding shocked.

"Well, I thought about quitting school and getting a job myself," Cassidy said. "Do you know anyone who would hire a thirteen-year-old?"

"You're kidding!" Katie said. "Cassidy, you can't quit school." She looked at her incredulously.

"Of course I'm kidding," Cassidy said, laughing a little through her tears. She wiped at her eyes with the back of her hand. "But if I really thought it would help my parents, I would get a job."

"You said they might have to sell her," Dylan pointed out. "Maybe they won't have to. She won today. If she keeps on winning, maybe they'll make enough money."

Cassidy shook her head. "I think it's a pretty big maybe," she said quietly. "My dad's not doing well with his new job. I heard him say so." She sighed. "If only there was some way he could get back into the horse business."

Dylan came over and sat down beside her on the arm of the couch. He put his arm across her shoulders, but he didn't say anything. There was nothing to say.

"Hey, didn't you just go to a big show in New York a few weeks ago?" Katie asked. "How did your family afford it?"

"I don't know," Cassidy said miserably. "I thought everything was okay until pretty recently. I had been training for that show for so long. I guess my parents didn't want me to know they were having problems with money, so they went ahead and paid for the show." Now that she thought about it, she felt terribly guilty. "I had no idea things were so bad, or I never would have gone," she said bitterly.

"Wow," Christina said. "I thought you were, like, rich or something."

"What'd you think that for?" Cassidy asked. Her eyes were still red but she had managed to stop crying.

Christina shrugged. "You're always wearing such nice clothes."

"You have two horses," Katie said.

"You talked about going to all those big, A-rated shows," Melanie added. "Showing is expensive."

"I thought your dad was some big banker or some-thing," Katie mused.

"I guess . . . I guess I was trying to make you all think my family was well-off," Cassidy admitted.

"But why?" Melanie asked.

Cassidy looked around at them all. "At the barn where I trained in Miami, if your parents weren't rich, you were a nobody," she said slowly. "Nobody would talk to you. I guess I thought it would be the same here."

"You think I'm friends with you because I thought your family had lots of money?" Dylan asked incredu-lously.

"Well, no, not really," Cassidy assured him.

"But you thought you had to impress us?" Christina asked, frowning.

"Well, you guys were so hard to get to know at first," Cassidy said.

"That's because you acted like such a snob!" Christina exclaimed.

"I was trying so hard to impress you guys, I guess I ended up looking like a jerk," Cassidy said, feeling foolish. "I'm sorry. Really I am."

There was a pause. Then Christina smiled at her. "No hard feelings." She went over to Cassidy and took her hand. "Friends?" she said.

Cassidy looked at Christina gratefully. It would be a relief not to have to pretend that everything was okay. "Friends," she said smiling.

They were all commiserating over Cassidy's bad luck when the kitchen door open with a bang. Christina's parents came in. Tall, blond Michael Reese peered into the living room.

"Hey, guys," Mike said. His face looked tired, but his blue eyes twinkled cheerfully. Then he frowned. "Why all the gloomy faces?" he asked.

"Cassidy's dad might have to—" Christina started to say.

"Oh, please don't say anymore about it," Cassidy begged. She was embarrassed enough as it was. She didn't need even more people shaking their heads over her family's predicament.

Christina gave her a perplexed look. "I think we should tell my mom and dad," she said. "They know an awful lot about the horse business. Maybe they can help."

"Help with what?" her father asked.

"Christina's right, Cassidy," Dylan said. "You should let them know what's going on."

"What is going on?" Ashleigh said, looking curiously at the kids.

Christina turned to Cassidy. "Is it okay if I tell them?" she asked. Christina actually seemed to want to help her.

"I guess so," Cassidy said.

"Mom, Cassidy's parents can't afford to pay the board and bills on Lady T anymore. They might have to sell her."

Cassidy saw Mike and Ashleigh exchange looks.

"Is there anything we could do?" Christina asked.

"Could they keep Lady T here?" Melanie asked.

"Her dad gets his suspension lifted next month," Kevin said. "Do you think my dad could hire him as an assistant trainer?"

Cassidy was touched at how much everybody seemed to care. She didn't really expect Christina's parents to be able to do anything, but it was a relief not to be worrying all alone anymore. Cassidy was glad she'd told them after all, she decided.

"What about it, Mom? Dad?" Christina persisted. "There must be something we can do."

Ashleigh and Mike were looking at each other again. They were both smiling. "I think maybe something's already been done," Ashleigh said mysteriously.

"What do you mean?" Melanie demanded.

"Well, I was just on the phone with Lee Miles, out in

California. Do you know who Lee Miles is?" Ashleigh asked.

Nobody had ever heard of him. "He's a trainer at Santa Anita Park, in Arcadia," Ashleigh said, then waited for a response.

"So what about him," Christina asked.

"He trains a very famous colt," Ashleigh hinted. "You were talking about him earlier?"

"Oh! I know—he trains Pizzazz!" Melanie guessed.

"Right," Mike said.

"Well, what about him?" Melanie asked.

Mike and Ashleigh exchanged looks again. Again Cassidy noticed the mysterious smiles and couldn't help feeling curious.

"Mr. Miles was inquiring about our farm. He wanted to know if we had a few stalls available," Mike said. "It seems there's going to be a very big race at Keeneland in two weeks."

Cassidy knew that Keeneland was the big racetrack in Lexington, about ten miles away. "What race?" she asked curiously.

"It's going to be a match race," Ashleigh said. "Between Pizzazz and a certain talented filly that we know." She raised an eyebrow, waiting for someone to guess.

"Lady T?" Cassidy asked.

"That's right," Mike said. "The media has been practically begging for a match race between "The California King" and "The Queen of the East," as they're known in the racing papers. When Lady T won the Ruffian Handicap today, that got everyone going again. The public is clamoring for a contest between the colt and the filly—and it looks like they're going to get one."

"A match race!" Melanie exclaimed. "That's totally cool!"

"I was also on the phone with Frank Taylor," Ashleigh said.

"Mr. Taylor trains Lady T," Cassidy told the kids.

Ashleigh went on. "Both Lady T and Pizzazz are going to be boarded here at Whitebrook for the next couple of weeks."

"Lady T's coming here? To Whitebrook?" Cassidy was trying to be calm, but she couldn't keep the excitement from creeping into her voice.

Mike nodded. "They didn't want the horses to stay at Keeneland, because of all the reporters and fans that will be hanging around there," he explained.

"Cassidy, do you know what this race means for your dad?" Ashleigh asked.

Cassidy shook her head. She didn't know, but she had a feeling it couldn't be bad.

"It means your dad is going to make a whole lot of money, as long as nothing happens between now and race time," Mike said, chuckling.

"How much will he get?" Dylan asked.

"Two hundred and fifty thousand dollars goes to the winner," Mike said.

"Oh, I hope Lady T does win," Katie said.

"Me too," Mike said. "But even if Lady T loses, her owner will get paid a hundred and fifty thousand dollars," he went on.

"They get that much money for losing?" Christina said incredulously. "Maybe when I grow up I'll get into the racing business after all."

Mike laughed. "It's nice work if you can get it," he said.

The phone rang again. Ashleigh picked it up and spoke briefly. When she hung up, she said, "Dylan, that was your mom calling on her cell phone. She's waiting outside."

"Okay. Thanks for the pizza," Dylan said.

"Yes, thank you very much," Katie said politely.

Cassidy thanked Christina's mom, then added, "And thanks for the great news!"

"You're welcome," Ashleigh said cheerfully.

Cassidy, Dylan, and Katie said good-bye, then headed outside where Dylan's mom was waiting in the van. Cassidy couldn't stop smiling. The match race was a solution she'd never thought of; her parents either, she guessed. But maybe it really would solve all their problems. For the first time in weeks, she actually began to feel hopeful. And for the first time since moving to Kentucky, she was actually happy to be going home.

Weekends usually went by way too fast, but this time it seemed to take forever to get to Monday. All day at school, Cassidy kept thinking that time must have slowed down. Finally the dismissal bell rang and soon Cassidy was standing in the parking area outside the stables at Whitebrook, waiting anxiously for Lady T to arrive.

"Oh, where are they?" Cassidy said for the twelfth time. She glanced at her watch. "I thought they would be here by now." She had ridden home with Christina and Melanie on the school bus so that she could be there when the horse arrived. Melanie and Christina were waiting with her.

"Maybe they're just driving really slowly and carefully," Christina said, trying to sound reassuring. "You know how these country roads are. I bet they'll show up any minute."

"I don't know. . . ." Melanie shook her head. "They might have gotten lost. What if they got here before we came home from school, and then they accidentally went into the stallion barn? If they ran into Mr. Ballard, it could be—" she paused dramatically, "—too late."

Mr. Ballard was the manager of the stallion barn at Whitebrook. Cassidy had never met him, but she had heard all about him from the other kids. It was rumored that Mr. Ballard had once been in prison. Christina swore that he would chase kids with a lunge whip if he caught them messing around in his barn. Even Melanie, who was known to be fearless at facing adults, stayed away from Mr. Ballard. She began to act out an imaginary drama.

"Hey, what a pretty horse," Melanie drawled, pretending to be the truck driver. "Can I pet him?" She reached out a hand and then recoiled in mock horror. "Oh my gosh, it's . . . The Terminator!" The Terminator, Cassidy knew, was a particularly aggressive stallion owned by Whitebrook.

Melanie let out a strangled cry, pretending to be pummeled and then trampled by a maniac horse, while Cassidy and Christina regarded her with amusement. After an elaborate death scene, Melanie flopped on the ground, then squinted up at them. "Tomorrow, the headlines read: TRUCK DRIVER AND TWO HORSES TORN TO SHREDS! PSYCHOTIC BARN MANAGER LETS KILLER STUD ATTACK! MORE ON PAGE TWO." She dropped once more and lay in a limp heap on the gravel.

A moment later, Kevin McLean strolled out of the yearling barn, where Lady T was going to be stabled. He saw Melanie lying inert and looked curiously at the other girls. "What's up with her?" Kevin asked, gesturing at Melanie.

Christina rolled her eyes. "Mel's obviously missed her calling. She should be an actress. You can get up now, Melanie," she added.

But Melanie continued to lie there. Cassidy saw Kevin slip back into the barn. She wondered what he was up to.

"Come on, Mel, get up," Christina said again, nudging her cousin with the toe of her paddock boot.

Melanie remained motionless. Kevin came back with a red plastic bucket he'd taken from just inside the barn door.

"What are you—?" Cassidy started to say.

Kevin shushed her soundlessly with a finger on his lips. He took the bucket and began quietly scooping up water from a galvanized-tin trough outside the barn. He tiptoed toward Melanie, trying not to slosh the water around. Cassidy had to stifle a giggle, as she realized what was about to happen. Kevin, grinning from ear to ear, sneaked up to where Melanie lay, still pretending to be unconscious. He held the bucket poised over her face for a moment, drawing out the suspense.

Christina, who had been shaking with silent laughter, let out a snort. At the same time, a droplet of water splashed on Melanie's nose, and she opened her eyes. "Oh, no you don't!" she exclaimed, trying to squirm out of the way. But she wasn't quick enough.

"Oh, yes I do!" Kevin said. He doused her with the bucket of water, soaking her head and one shoulder. Then he stood back, laughing as he waited for Melanie's response.

"Kevin!" Melanie exclaimed. She scrambled up, sputtering, and lunged at him, but Kevin dodged her easily and ran to the trough for a second bucketful. Melanie looked around and spied another bucket sitting just outside the barn. She grabbed it and sunk it into the trough to fill it, then went after Kevin.

"Get him, Melanie!" Cassidy cheered, as she and Christina backed out of the line of fire.

Kevin unloaded his bucket in Melanie's direction, but this time barely splashed her. "Uh-oh," he said, looking with dismay at his empty bucket. He glanced hopefully toward the trough, but Melanie was between it and Kevin.

"Ha! I've got you now," Melanie said. She came after him, her bucket full, a gleam in her eye.

"Watch out, Kevvy," Christina warned.

Kevin dropped the bucket and backed away as Melanie advanced. Suddenly he ducked behind Cassidy and Christina, just as Melanie slung the contents of her bucket at him.

"Oh!" Cassidy gasped, as the cold water hit her right in the face.

"Melanie!" Christina yelled, water streaming off her clothes.

"Sorry!" Melanie said, giggling helplessly. "Not!"

"Good shot, Melanie!" Kevin teased.

"I'll get you," Christina promised, grabbing the bucket Kevin had dropped and running for the water trough.

Somehow Cassidy found herself in the middle of a water fight. She didn't have a bucket, so she just used her hand to splash water from the trough on anyone who came near her. In few minutes, she was as soaked as everyone else and having a great time. The weather was still hot, so the water felt good. And it felt even better to be playing around, having fun. She was so distracted she didn't even notice the horse transport van until, with a hiss and a rattle, engines rumbling, it started up the long gravel driveway.

"Oh my gosh! They're here!" Cassidy said, when she did see the truck.

"Truce!" Melanie called. "Everyone drop your weapons," she ordered. "Kevin."

Reluctantly he set down his bucket. "Okay, okay," he muttered.

The big truck lumbered up the driveway and maneuvered into position with a lot of squeaking brakes and crunching gravel. With a last hydraulic hiss and sigh, it rolled to a stop and the driver cut the engines. Christina's dad came out of the barn office to oversee unloading the horse. Moments later, the driver had pulled the ramp down and a handler came off the truck leading a comely bay Thoroughbred with a pretty little white star on her broad forehead.

"Lady T!" Cassidy said joyfully. She grabbed one hand with the other, dying to get her hands on the filly's satiny neck, but knowing better than to run up and startle her.

"Wow, she's gorgeous," Melanie said in awe.

"She sure is," Cassidy said proudly.

A car had followed the truck up the driveway. Two men got out, one in khakis and a red polo shirt, the other wearing a navy blazer with some kind of badge clipped onto the breast pocket.

"Who are those guys?" Melanie asked.

"I think the guy in the red shirt is Frank Taylor, the trainer," Cassidy said. "I met him once." *Dad should be training her,* she thought, sadly.

"The guy in the blazer is a detective, I bet you any-thing," Kevin said quietly. "Look, see that lump under his coat? I bet it's a gun."

"A gun! What would he need that for?" Christina scoffed. "This is just a horse farm. There aren't going to be any crimes around here."

"It's probably just a walkie-talkie," Melanie sug-gested.

They watched as the two men conferred for a moment. Then the man in khakis spoke to Mike.

Cassidy focused on Lady T. The handler was just holding her by the lead shank, letting her get a look around after being in the dim trailer for so many hours. The filly had a petite head, with a dainty muzzle and ears and a well-formed shoulder that blended into the perfect curve of her neck. Her face was still babyish, but her eyes seemed calm and wise as they regarded her new surroundings.

"Okay, let's go, little girl," the handler said, clucking a little to get the filly moving.

"Bring her right in here," Mike said, showing the handler the way. "Her stall's all ready."

The handler led the horse down the aisle after Mike and the two other men. Cassidy, Christina, Melanie, and Kevin followed right behind. They knew better than to get in the way; even Mike would have shooed them right out of the barn if they came one step too close. The handler was looking suspiciously at them already. But the kids instinctively kept just enough of a respectful distance that nobody could really get after them.

They watched as the filly was led into her stall and her shipping wraps were removed.

"She's so pretty," Melanie whispered.

"She looks bigger than the last time I saw her," Cassidy whispered back.

"You guys, this isn't the library," Christina said aloud. "Melanie, you're acting like you never saw a racehorse before. I don't see what the big deal is."

"Christina, this isn't just any racehorse," Melanie countered.

"Yeah," Kevin agreed. "She's, like, the Queen of England of racehorses."

"Ooh, the queen," Christina said in a mock-queenly falsetto. "Helloo! Helloo!" She began waving as if she were surrounded by crowds, a tiny, formal wave with her fingers held stiffly together as if she were a traveling dignitary. "Make way for the Queen of Racehorses!"

Cassidy and Melanie had to laugh. The man in the navy blazer finally seemed to notice them. He strolled over to the kids, frowning. "Hey, what are you kids doing hanging around in here?" he said.

Cassidy tried to think of some kind of response that wouldn't immediately get them kicked out of the barn. But Melanie spoke first.

"We live here," Melanie said, squaring off with all four feet, nine inches of her height to look the man boldly in the eye. "What about you?"

The man was broad-shouldered and heavyset, and

about as old as her father, Cassidy guessed. His eyes narrowed in his red face as he met Melanie's gaze. He put a hand on his hip, pulling back his blazer to reveal what was indeed a gun in a black leather holster. Cassidy gasped and took a step back. Kevin gave her an elbow and a look that said, "I told you so." Even Melanie, who wasn't afraid of anyone, looked shocked for a split second when she saw the gun.

Cassidy didn't like conflict, and she was sure she was about to be involved in some. Melanie, she had learned, had a knack for stirring up trouble. Then, to her surprise, the man's fierce expression changed. He burst out with a hearty chuckle as he continued to regard Melanie with his blue eyes, which were now twinkling with friendliness.

"You got some guts, kid," he laughed. "What's your name?"

"What's your name?" Melanie countered.

"Okay, fair enough," the man said. "I'm Charlie McGowan, from the Briggs Detective Agency." He stuck out his hand to shake Melanie's.

"I'm Melanie Graham," Melanie said, grasping his huge hand with her tiny one.

Cassidy, Christina, and Kevin introduced themselves. "Call me Charlie," he said, shaking hands with each one of them.

"Are you a private investigator?" Kevin asked eagerly.

Charlie nodded. "I used to be a New York City

homicide detective. I'm retired from that. I've been working around racehorses for about ten years now. If you're worried about that little lady," he said, nodding toward Lady T, "she's safe with me. Cross my heart," he promised, criss-crossing his chest with one finger.

"Why should we be worried?" Cassidy asked uneasily. "What could happen?"

"Oh, you know, it's a big deal, this race," Charlie said. "These are two very famous, very valuable horses. There are going to be reporters all over the place. And curiosity seekers. You know how people are. They can't stay away from celebrities, horses included. Don't look so worried, sweetheart," he said to Cassidy. "They won't get too close with me."

"Cassidy's dad owns Lady T," Melanie informed Charlie.

"Is that a fact? Well, she's going to make a lot of money for him if she wins," Charlie said. "But she's got some competition, I understand. Say, did that other horse get here yet? The colt, Pizzazz?"

"Not yet," Christina told him. "They're due in tomorrow."

Charlie nodded. "It's a long way from California. I guess they must think he's going to win, if they shipped him that far."

"Who do you think is going to win?" Melanie asked.

Charlie smiled at Cassidy. "Oh, I'm for your filly all the way. And I got a knack for picking winners."

Cassidy smiled back at him. She hoped he was right.

7

"CAMPBELL . . ." CASSIDY WHISPERED. "CAMPBELL, WAKE UP."

Cassidy's older brother rolled over, wrapping the covers around him, and shoved his head under the pillow. Cassidy nudged him. "Campbell," she said a little louder. He didn't stir. She glanced at the digital clock beside his bed. The blue-green numbers said 5:05. It was Friday morning. She had spent the last three days convincing her brother to agree to drive her to Whitebrook early that morning, so she could watch the two famous horses' workouts. Then she would take the bus to school with Kevin, Christina, and Melanie. But if she didn't get there soon, she'd miss the workouts. She studied her sleeping brother for a moment, then pulled the pillow off his head. "Campbell. Wake up," she repeated.

Campbell opened one eye and glared sleepily at his

sister. "Go away," he mumbled, groping for the pillow.

Cassidy hid it behind her back. "Come on, there isn't much time," she said.

"Torturing your brother when sleeping is a capital offense," Campbell commented. "I'm going to have to kill you. Prepare to die. As soon as I get up." He glanced at the clock. "In two and a half more hours." He pulled the covers over his head.

Cassidy promptly pulled them off again. "You promised to drive me to Whitebrook this morning," she reminded him.

"I was delirious," Campbell said. "No one could possibly get up this early." He grabbed the pillow and burrowed his head underneath it.

Cassidy pulled the pillow off. "You promised," she insisted. "Remember? I'm going to do your dishes for a whole week." She waited.

Campbell gave a groan of pain. "How do I get myself into these things?" he muttered. "I must be crazy." But he sat up, yawning hugely and rubbing at his eyes.

"Here," Cassidy said, tossing him the jeans and T-shirt he'd worn the day before. "Hurry up! If we don't get there soon, I'll miss the workouts."

A short while later Cassidy had finally arrived at Whitebrook, anxious that she was later than she'd planned to be. "Thanks, Campbell," she told her brother.

Campbell grunted something in reply, but Cassidy didn't stop to hear what it was. With a glance toward the stables, she shouldered her backpack and hurried down to the training oval.

Several horses were on the track, jogging or galloping. Cassidy set her backpack on the grass and leaned against the fence, searching for Lady T. She was disappointed that the filly was nowhere in sight. Then Cassidy spotted Melanie on her big, black gelding, Pirate Treasure. Melanie saw Cassidy and gave her a wave. Cassidy waved back. *Seeing Melanie at work ponying the racehorses is a lot different from seeing her in the jump class at Mona's,* Cassidy thought. On Trib, Melanie always looked a little unsure of herself. On Pirate, Melanie looked as calm and professional as the exercise riders up on the fancy, swift Thoroughbreds.

Cassidy watched Melanie escort a sweaty chestnut horse out the gap. Then Melanie trotted Pirate over to her. "Hi," Melanie said.

"Hi," Cassidy answered. "You look great up there," she told her.

"Thanks," Melanie said modestly, sliding her hand down Pirate's shiny, black neck.

The big horse gave a low snort, almost like a cat purring. "Hi, handsome," Cassidy said to him. She looked up at Melanie. "Can I pet him?" she asked.

"Of course," Melanie said.

Cassidy reached over the rail and stroked Pirate's neck and shoulder. "He is such a cool horse, Melanie,"

Cassidy said admiringly. "The way he acts, you'd never know he's blind. Is he fun to ride?"

"The best," Melanie said beaming. "He's sooo smooth. Maybe you can try him out sometime," she offered.

"That'd be great," Cassidy said.

"How come you're so late?" Melanie wanted to know.

"I couldn't get my brother out of bed," Cassidy said. "I'll be so glad when I'm old enough to drive. Did I miss Lady T's workout?"

Melanie nodded. "She got out really early. But Pizzazz hasn't worked yet—hey, here he comes. Look."

Cassidy looked in the direction Melanie was pointing and saw the big chestnut colt stepping onto the training track, his white socks flashing in the morning sunlight. She'd managed to get a look at him in his stall a couple of days ago, right after he'd arrived. But unlike Charlie McGowan and most of the staff attending Lady T, the security guards and grooms around Pizzazz's stall in the main barn were surly and secretive. They didn't want anyone near the colt and had actually demanded that the barn be sectioned off so that only their staff was allowed to use that end of it.

Cassidy had really been hoping to see Lady T gallop, but she watched with interest as Pizzazz's exercise rider began to jog him the wrong way, clockwise, around the track. The colt was much bigger-boned than Lady T. The morning sun highlighted his muscular haunches and flamed in his coppery coat. Cassidy turned her head, and Melanie turned in the saddle to watch him as he pranced by. He was supreme, as excellent a colt as Lady T was perfection in a filly, and Cassidy felt a thrill of excitement as she thought of the upcoming match race. It would truly be a test of champions.

The colt had jogged around to the far side of the track. Cassidy saw him walk and then turn around. A moment later he was galloping up the backstretch, smooth and swift, like a silk scarf blown by the wind. He rounded the turn and then headed down the homestretch toward Cassidy and Melanie.

"Look at his face," Melanie said. "He wants to go."

Cassidy understood. The colt was tossing his head impatiently as his legs pounded the dirt. He looked as if he wanted to toss the bridle off and be free to run, unrestricted by rider or tack. But his exercise rider, with a grim look of concentration, was holding him back. This was just a workout, just a little gallop to keep the horse fit. Cassidy knew they would save the colt's real speed for the race.

Then, just as Pizzazz drew even with Cassidy and Melanie, something went wrong. The colt's head had been up, fighting the bit as he galloped on. Suddenly his head dropped, and he broke stride and stumbled.

"Oh, no," Cassidy said, her heart doing a double flop.

"Oh, gosh. What happened?" Melanie said, almost at the same time.

Pizzazz looked for a moment as though he would go down. Cassidy gasped. A horse that stumbled going that fast would surely be injured or throw his rider. But the colt dug in with his hind legs and managed to get his front feet under him again. The rider, too, managed to keep his seat.

"Whoa, son," the rider said, pulling back on the reins to stop the colt.

Pizzazz had slowed, but still seemed to want to run. The rider was slowly increasing his hold on the reins, gradually slowing the colt, who seemed almost annoyed at the interruption in his work. But when he finally broke into a trot, Cassidy could tell that something wasn't right.

"Look, he's lame," Melanie said.

"Oh, no," Cassidy said again, her heart sinking. *If Pizzazz is lame they'll have to call off the race. There'll be no winner, no loser, and no prize money for anybody. And Dad will lose Lady T!* Cassidy thought. She gripped the rail with her hands so hard her knuckles were white. "Please be all right, please be all right," she whispered over and over to herself.

"He might need ponying back to the barn," Melanie said. She moved Pirate out into the track and trotted cautiously toward Pizzazz. "Need some help?" she asked the exercise rider, who was still wrestling to hold Pizzazz back. The horse was fighting him every second, still trying to run, although he was obviously limping.

"Get away, kid," the rider snapped, see-sawing the

bit in Pizzazz's mouth. The horse flipped his head up, foam flying. Just then a pony and rider from Pizzazz's stable got to his side. The exercise rider jumped off the colt as the pony rider grabbed Pizzazz's reins and began leading him off the track. The beautiful horse had calmed down with the pony by his side, though he was limping significantly, clearly in pain from one of his front legs. Cassidy thought he looked perplexed that his workout was ending in such a strange way. But he walked willingly beside the pony, who escorted him down the track toward the gap. The exercise rider gave a look over his shoulder, frowned at Cassidy and Melanie, then turned and began striding back toward the gap after the colt.

Melanie trotted back toward Cassidy. "Boy, what a grouch," she said.

"What do you think is wrong with Pizzazz?" Cassidy asked anxiously.

Melanie shook her head. "I don't know. Maybe he just took a bad step and he'll work out of it."

"I sure hope that's all it is," Cassidy said. But as she looked up toward the stables, where Pizzazz's hindquarter was just vanishing into the barn, she was full of doubt.

Melanie glanced at her watch. "I've got to put Pirate away. I'll meet you at the bottom of the driveway in half an hour, okay?"

"Okay," Cassidy nodded. She shouldered her backpack and trudged up the hill, then down the long gravel driveway to the bus stop. There she sat down on the grass to wait for Melanie, Christina, Kevin, and the school bus.

Henry Clay Middle School in Lexington was actually a lot like Cassidy's school in Miami. The kids acted pretty much the same and dressed pretty much the same. *It could have been a lot worse,* Cassidy reflected. She'd been relieved and a little surprised to discover that, of all the rotten things she'd had to deal with lately, school hadn't been one of them. Eighth graders were the upperclassmen, so she didn't have to worry about getting picked on by older kids. And she was glad that they had started doing algebra in math. Christina, who was in Cassidy's class, didn't like it much, but Cassidy was great at math and enjoyed the challenge.

That day though, Cassidy couldn't seem to concentrate on anything, even algebra. The hot weather made the un–air-conditioned classrooms sticky and close, and the desks were uncomfortable no matter how she changed positions. Over and over her gaze drifted from the work in front of her to the window, which overlooked the front parking lot of the school. She gnawed at her pencil, mulling over the incident with Pizzazz that morning.

What had been strange about it? She went over the events in her head, just as she remembered them. Pizzazz had come onto the track. He had jogged around, warming up. Then his rider had turned him to the left and galloped him. The colt had been fighting for his head all the way, but the rider kept him firmly in hand.

Then Pizzazz had stumbled and pulled up, limping. Had the rider interfered so much that he caused the horse to trip? Cassidy doubted it. No trainer would put an amateur up on a horse like Pizzazz. For a race as important as the match race, the horse's regular exercise rider and grooms would travel with him. An experienced rider who knew the horse well and had exercised him many times wouldn't be likely to ride him so poorly that he tripped the colt.

The colt definitely hadn't spooked or bucked. Cassidy remembered the determined look in his eye as he charged down the stretch in a steady gallop as fast as his rider would allow. She tried to remember if there had been anything on the track that could have caused Pizzazz to stumble. But the weeks of clear, hot weather had left the track flat and firm, the footing good. Cassidy couldn't see any reason for the stumble. And then she wondered, *Did the stumble cause the colt's injury*, as she had thought at first? Or was it the other way around? *Did Pizzazz have some kind of weakness or injury that had made him stumble?*

When the last bell rang, Cassidy jumped as if she'd been shocked. Her knee thumped the bottom of the desk painfully. She glanced around, rubbing her knee and hoping no one had noticed. Joey Gillis, who sat across from her, gave her an amused look. He was holding his books under one arm, looking hopefully at her as if he wanted to talk, but Cassidy ignored him. She was much too preoccupied to think about boys. She gathered up her books and headed for the door, grateful that the school day was over. Tomorrow was Saturday. Maybe she could talk her dad into driving her to Whitebrook early to watch Lady T work out. She had tried all week to get him to come and see the filly, but he wouldn't. "It's best if I stay away, under the circumstances," he'd told her. "That way, if anything happens, nobody can connect me with it at all." *If anything happens.* Cassidy had just closed her locker and started down the hall when she heard Melanie calling her.

"Hey, Cassidy, wait up," Melanie said.

Cassidy stopped. Melanie and Christina caught up with her and the three of them began walking out to board the bus.

"You're going to jump class, right?" Melanie asked.

"Oh my gosh!" Cassidy thumped the side of her head with one hand. "I totally forgot to remind my brother," Cassidy said. "I hope he's home when I get there."

"Why don't you ride home with us?" Melanie suggested. "Then we can all walk over to Mona's. You have chaps and stuff over there, right?"

Cassidy nodded. It made sense to take the school bus to Whitebrook. Then she wouldn't have to depend on Campbell to drive her.

"Hey, want to sleep over at our house tonight?" Melanie asked her.

"Sure!" Cassidy exclaimed. Perfect! She could get up early in the morning and be sure to catch the workouts.

"Great," Melanie said. "So just come on home with us."

"Oh, except, I don't have any clothes or a toothbrush or anything," Cassidy remembered.

"I can lend you something to wear," Christina offered. "And I'm sure Mom has an extra toothbrush around somewhere."

Cassidy looked curiously at Christina, but she seemed sincere. And Cassidy knew she could fit into Christina's clothes. Once she had lent Christina her riding clothes and they'd discovered that they were exactly the same size, except Christina's foot was a half-size bigger.

"Okay," Cassidy said. "You're sure it'll be okay with your mom?"

"Don't worry," Christina confirmed. "We asked her this morning. What about your mom? Do you need to call her?"

Cassidy nodded. "I can call her from your house. She won't mind. . . . In fact, she probably won't even notice," Cassidy said.

"How come?" Melanie asked.

Cassidy sighed. "She's been really distracted lately. I guess she's just preoccupied, with all the problems we've been having lately. You know what she did last week?" Cassidy went on. "She took me to the mall to get some school supplies, and we were supposed to meet back at the front entrance after she ran an errand. Only she forgot to pick me up."

"You're kidding," Christina said. "What'd you do?"

"I walked home," Cassidy said with a shrug. "It's not that far."

"That's terrible," Melanie said.

"It doesn't sound that bad," Christina said. "There have been times when I've wished my mom would forget about me," she joked.

"Anyway, I'm sure I can spend the night," Cassidy said, as she followed Christina and Melanie onto the school bus. "Mom won't mind."

At Whitebrook, Cassidy called her mom at work and got permission to sleep over. Then she walked out to the main barn and helped Melanie get Trib ready for the lesson at Mona's. When they finished, Christina was still working on Sterling. But Cassidy knew that Sterling was particular about who handled her, and Christina liked to do things her own way, so she didn't offer to help. Melanie sat down on a trunk to wait, while Cassidy wandered down to the far end of the barn to check on Lady T.

The filly wasn't in her stall, and Charlie McGowan was nowhere around either. Cassidy guessed that Frank or Julio, Lady T's groom, would be grazing her somewhere. Cassidy stepped outside and looked around for the filly, but she didn't see her. Then she decided to go and see if she could take a peek at Pizzazz.

She walked around to the end of the barn where the colt was stabled and peered cautiously inside. The colt was in the aisle, being held by a groom, while several men stood around him. Cassidy recognized Lee Miles, the colt's trainer. Two men in business suits stood nearby, while another man was squatting down, his hands on Pizzazz's left front leg. Cassidy wasn't sure what he was doing. Then Cassidy spotted a bag and some medical equipment, and a few used cotton balls soaked with brown antiseptic, and she realized he must be a veterinarian.

None of the men had noticed her. Cassidy stood just outside the doorway of the barn, peeking in and straining to hear the conversation.

"Well, what's it look like?" Mr. Miles was saying.

The vet, a tall thin man with graying hair and wire-rimmed glasses, stood up, but he continued to look at the horse's leg. "Well, it's pretty clear from the ultra-sound. It's the same old problem."

"Well, it's never bothered him this much before," one of the other men argued. "He's got to run. Isn't there something you can give him?"

"The horse needs rest," the vet said. "He can't run like this."

"He has to! We can't pull out now. The race is only a week away," the first owner protested. "Give him something."

"But if it's illegal . . ." the second man said, sounding doubtful. "This isn't Lasix we're talking about."

Cassidy knew they must be talking about some kind of drug. Any winning race horse would immediately have his urine collected and tested for drugs. A few drugs, such as Lasix, which could keep a horse's lungs from bleeding, were allowed. Any illegal drugs detected in the horse's blood or urine would disqualify him. She listened more intently.

"We can work around that," the first man said. Cassidy guessed he must be one of the owners. "Some of those drugs you inject right into the joint, so they don't show up in the urine sample. Right, Doc?"

"Yeah, but you don't run a horse like that! You rest him," the vet protested. "This is a valuable animal. You don't want to break him down at this point in his career, do you?"

"It's only one race," the first owner said. "And it's only a week away."

"Yeah, couldn't we give him a little something for the match race and then try resting him?" the second owner asked. "I mean, if he's been going like this all along, it doesn't seem like it would hurt him to run one more time. As long as he's not in pain."

"Oh, sure, we can stop the pain. And he'll run this race all right," the vet said. "But you're taking a mighty big chance."

Mr. Miles glanced up toward the doorway, and Cassidy ducked out of the way just in time. *Poor Pizzazz!*

Cassidy had been right. *The horse* did *have an injury. But what was wrong with him? And what were they going to give him?* She wished the vet would say more. Cautiously she peeked back around the edge of the doorway.

". . . do you recommend we do?" Mr. Miles was asking.

"Well, he might hold up, or he might not," the vet said. "I'd call off the race if I were you."

Call off the race? "Oh, no," Cassidy whispered to herself, stricken. If they called off the race, there would be no prize money. And Lady T would have to be sold. The two owners and the trainer had withdrawn into a little group, and they conferred quietly. Cassidy waited to hear what they would say. *Would they call off the race?* She wished the vet had said more about the injury, whatever it was. Then Mr. Miles turned to face the vet.

"They want to run him, Sam," he said calmly.

"It's a bad idea. If he stops now, we can fix him. If he runs . . ." The vet shook his head.

The men were holding out some papers for the vet to sign. "Right here, Doc," the first owner was saying.

The vet stared at the papers. Slowly he raised a hand and laid it against Pizzazz's shoulder as if he were going to pat him, but he didn't. He just rested his hand there. Then he picked up his bag and equipment and started toward the doorway. Cassidy had to scramble behind some decorative hedges growing outside the barn. The hedges weren't very big; she crouched down and hoped they would be enough cover.

"Hey, what's he doing?" she heard one of the owners say angrily. "Where do you think you're going? We need you to sign the vet approval on these papers for him to enter the race."

"That's right, you do," the vet said, heading for his truck.

Cassidy had been hoping she could question the vet about Pizzazz's condition, but the owners followed him out to the truck. Mr. Miles went as far as the doorway of the barn and stood watching. Cassidy dropped to her hands and knees behind the hedge and began to crawl along the wall toward the corner of the barn. "C'mon, Doc," the first owner demanded. "Don't be ridiculous. You've got to sign. Here." He held out the papers to the vet.

The vet simply ignored him. He opened the back door of the truck and began setting his equipment inside. Cassidy crawled around the corner where she had a better view and was safely out of sight of Mr. Miles.

"Lee, talk some sense into him, will you?" one of the men said. "He has to sign them."

"No, I don't," the vet said coolly. "You're asking me to put my signature on a piece of paper that says the horse is fit to run, when I know he isn't. I won't do it; I don't care how much money it's worth." He got in the truck and slammed the door.

"Hey, Doc, listen to reason, will you?" the man tried cajoling him. He leaned against the truck, speaking

93

through the open window. "You've always been our vet. Don't back out on us now."

"I approved the horse up to now because his condition was borderline, and he didn't seem to be getting worse," the vet said. "Well, now he's worse, and I'm not going to say he's fit. Find another vet to lie for you, if you can, and I hope you don't," he said firmly. "I know I'm through."

"Listen, you!" the owner said angrily. He reached through the window into the cab and grabbed the vet by the collar of his shirt, raising a fist as if he were threatening to punch him.

"Uh-oh," Cassidy said softly. She craned her head, trying to get a better view through the thick branches.

"Let go of me," the vet said coldly. Cassidy couldn't see his face, but he didn't sound at all afraid. The second owner grabbed the first owner and pulled him off.

The vet put the truck in gear and backed out of his parking spot. As the tail of the truck swung around toward her, Cassidy noticed the license plate. It was a California plate, with just a series of letters: DRSFINE. The vet headed down the driveway, leaving the owners standing in a small cloud of white dust. Cassidy watched the truck turn onto the main road and pull away, growing smaller and smaller until it vanished over a hill. She had a sinking feeling that the match race, and her father's chances of keeping Lady T, had just vanished along with it.

8

"WELL, NOW WHAT DO WE DO?" THE SECOND OWNER SAID, sounding very unsure.

"We find another vet, that's what we do," the first owner exclaimed. "I can tell you one thing, we're not calling off that race."

They went back to the barn, one stomping, the other following. Cassidy waited until she was sure the coast was clear, then she scrambled out of the hedge. *Wait'll I tell Melanie and Christina about this*, she thought. She was brushing the dirt from her hands and knees when someone clasped her shoulder in a firm grip.

Cassidy lunged forward, and let out a scream before she could stop herself. Then she covered her mouth with both hands and whirled around to confront who-ever had grabbed her. She expected to see one of Pizzazz's owners or Mr. Miles. To her relief, she saw the amused face of Charlie McGowan.

"Sorry, kid," he said. "I didn't mean to scare you, but what are you so jumpy for? You're not up to something are you?"

Cassidy shook her head and held a hand to her chest while she waited for her heart to stop thumping. "I—I just—these guys were having an argument," she finally got out. "And it was kind of scary, so I hid in the bushes."

"Where are they now?" Charlie asked her.

"One of them left," Cassidy said. "I think the other guys went back in the barn."

"What were they arguing about?" Charlie wanted to know.

Cassidy almost told him, then she thought better of it. After all, she didn't really know for sure what was wrong with the colt. Maybe it was just some kind of disagreement between the owners and the vet. "I'm not sure," Cassidy said innocently. "I think it was about signing some papers or something like that."

"Well, let me know if you hear anything else," Charlie said. "And stay out of the bushes will you? Somebody'll think you're up to no good. By the way, your friends are looking for you."

The jump class! Cassidy checked her watch. It was already after four. The class was supposed to start at four-thirty. "Oh, shoot!" Cassidy said. "I'm late!" She hurried around to the main barn, looking for Christina and Melanie. They had waited for her, but now they'd have to hurry to get to Mona's on time.

"Where were you?" Melanie asked, as they crossed a pasture and headed for the gate that separated Mona's land from Whitebrook. She and Christina were riding, and Cassidy was on foot.

Cassidy described the incident with the vet and the owners to the other girls. She had to walk fast to keep up with the long strides of the horses, so by the time she finished telling the story, she was breathless. "And then," she panted, "he just drove away," she finished.

"What did he say was actually wrong with the horse?" Christina asked.

Cassidy shook her head. "I don't know," she said. "He never did say. Whatever it is, it's some kind of condition that they've known about for a while. Apparently it's never caused problems until now. But I did hear him say that he didn't think the horse should run."

"So is the match race going to be called off?" Melanie asked.

"I don't know that either," Cassidy said. "I mean, obviously I hope it isn't, because of what it'll mean to my dad and my family. But on the other hand, I wouldn't want Pizzazz to run if it's going to hurt him."

"Maybe the vet was overreacting," Christina said. "Maybe it's just a little thing, like bucked shins. He might have some discomfort, but if he rests, it'll get better. And it's not going to cause permanent damage or anything."

"What are bucked shins?" Melanie asked.

"It's when a horse gets swollen and sore in his front legs, on the front of his cannon bones, from getting overworked," Christina explained. "It happens a lot in young horses. Mom says when a horse gets bucked shins, it needs to build up more bone."

"What do they do for it?" Melanie asked.

Christina shrugged. "Just let them rest, I think."

"Bucked shins," Cassidy said thoughtfully. "Hmm. The vet did say the horse needed rest." She felt a little better. "Maybe that's all it is."

When they finally reached Mona's, Christina and Melanie went right down to the ring. Cassidy had to go to the barn first and get Rebound ready. She hurried to the tack room to get her saddle, knowing she'd have to really scramble to make it before the jump class started. Luckily, Rebound had been groomed in the morning, so he wasn't too dirty. As it was, the other kids had already started the warm-up by the time she got down to the arena. Cassidy apologized to Mona for being late, waved at Dylan and Katie, and joined the group in trotting as soon as she had let Rebound stretch his legs at the walk.

Mona set up a really fun course for them to jump, and for the rest of the hour, Cassidy forgot about everything except how good it felt to be riding her horse. But that night at Christina and Melanie's, she began to worry about Pizzazz again.

She and Christina were sitting at the foot of Melanie's bed, talking. "If he doesn't have bucked shins, what could it be?" Cassidy asked.

"I don't know for sure, but there are lots of things he could have wrong with him," Christina said. "Why don't we ask my mom?"

"Maybe we shouldn't say anything until we know more," Cassidy said.

"I have an idea," Melanie said. "Let's get up early and see if he works. If he does, he's probably fine, right?"

"But they were talking about giving him some kind of drug, so he could run," Cassidy pointed out. "What if they started doing that already? We wouldn't know if he was okay or not."

"Well, we won't find out anything if we don't at least try to check it out. Let's just see what he looks like tomorrow. If we think anything is wrong, we'll tell Aunt Ashleigh. She'll know the right thing to do," Melanie said confidently.

"Ugh," Christina groaned. "Do we really have to get up and watch the workouts? It's so early," she complained.

"How else are we going to find out what's wrong with Pizzazz?" Melanie demanded. "Come on, it won't kill you to get up before dawn for a change."

"It might," Christina grumbled.

"Next topic," Melanie went on. "Guess what? Guess what Stacy Gillis told me?" Melanie said.

"What?" Christina asked.

Cassidy wasn't sure she wanted to know. Stacy Gillis was a cheerleader, head of the Glee Club, and president of the student council. She was also Joey Gillis's sister. She was a year younger but she'd skipped a grade, so she and Joey were both in the eighth grade.

"Stacy told me that she heard Joey telling Andrew Worth that he likes you," Melanie said dramatically.

"Me?" Cassidy asked.

Melanie nodded emphatically. "He's probably going to ask you to the homecoming dance."

"Stacy Gillis is a big gossip," Christina said. "You can't believe a word she says."

"Joey's her brother; she ought to know," Melanie retorted.

"Do you like Joey Gillis?" Christina asked Cassidy.

Cassidy thought about it. Joey Gillis was tall and quiet. He had brown curly hair and dark blue eyes. He was one of the best basketball players on the Henry Clay Hornets as well as a reliable receiver on the football team. He was as popular as his sister, but in a low-key kind of way, and he seemed intelligent in class, though Cassidy had never actually had a conversation with him. "I guess he's all right," Cassidy said warily.

"Good!" Melanie said. "I'll tell Stacy."

"Oh, no, please don't," Cassidy begged. "Promise me you won't, Melanie, please?"

"But why?" Melanie asked. "He just wants to know that you like him so he can ask you to the dance. He's so cute, and he's really popular. Don't you think they'd make a great couple, Christina?"

"Perfect," Christina agreed.

Cassidy suspected that Christina was only in favor of her going out with Joey so that there would be no chance of her going to the dance with Dylan. But the thought of going to a dance with anybody but her old boyfriend seemed impossible. "I just . . . I'm not really interested in dating anyone right now," Cassidy said to them. "I'm so busy with my horses. . . ." she paused.

Melanie laughed. "We're just talking about one dance! It's not like you have to marry the guy."

"So just tell us, would you go with him?" Christina pressed.

"Oooh," Cassidy groaned. "You guys are killing me. Okay. Maybe I would go to a dance with him," she said, mostly to shut them up. Whether she would actually go was another matter entirely. "One dance. But don't make this out to be some kind of big deal, okay? Now can we just drop it?" She yawned. "If we're going to get up early, we'd better get to sleep."

Melanie woke up Cassidy and Christina early, as they had planned. By five o'clock they had staked out the training oval. By six o'clock they had seen several of Whitebrook's horses gallop or breeze, but no Pizzazz.

Christina covered a yawn. "I knew I should have stayed in bed."

"I guess he's not going to run," Melanie said.

Cassidy put a hand on Melanie's arm. "Look, they're bringing Lady T down. Let's watch her work, then go see if we can find out anything about Pizzazz."

Lady T sauntered onto the track as if she were stepping into a warm bath. Unlike the colt, who had pranced and jigged excitedly when he hit the dirt, the filly walked up the track the wrong way with easy, cat-like strides, her neck stretched out to its full, gracious length, her head low. Her exercise rider looked as calm as the filly. He crouched almost lazily over the saddle, letting her take all the rein she wanted.

The filly picked up a jog as she reached the spot where the girls were gathered on the rail watching. Cassidy leaned eagerly over the rail, drinking in the sight of the beautiful filly. A flash of white saddle pad, a brief metal jingle as she played with the bit, a silky swish of her dark tail, and she was past.

The rider took the filly around to the far side of the track, then turned her around to the left. Cassidy watched, mesmerized as Lady T broke into a swift gallop, breezing up to the far turn. Pizzazz had seemed to attack the race track, beating the dirt surface with great, plunging strides. Lady T, like water, simply flowed. Her feet stirred up little puffs of dirt but hardly made a sound as the track seemed to channel her, streaming, to the mile pole. As her exercise rider let her gallop out, then stood in the irons and began slowing her, Cassidy had one thought, and it filled her with excitement: *She'll win.* The filly shook her head playfully as if she couldn't quite believe the workout was over so quickly. Cassidy watched her, thrilled. *If she runs against Pizzazz,* Cassidy thought, *Lady T will win.*

"Wow, does she look good," Melanie said.

"You think?" Cassidy asked eagerly. She couldn't help feeling proud of her father's filly. She wished he could come and see her.

"Definitely," Melanie said. "I bet she'll win the race."

Then Cassidy remembered what the vet had said about Pizzazz. "If there is a race," she said gloomily.

"How about we break for breakfast?" Christina suggested.

Melanie shook her head. "First we have some detective work to do. Come on."

The three girls walked up to the main barn where Pizzazz was stabled. Around the side of the barn, right beside the hedge where Cassidy had hidden, they stood trying to decide the best way to get into the barn.

"I say we just walk right in," Christina said. "After all, it is my mom and dad's farm. They can't kick me out."

"They can so kick you out," Melanie said. "They don't have to let anybody near the horse, and it's clear

103

they don't want to. But I think you're right about just walking in. We might find out more if we just go in and start looking around and asking questions than if we try to sneak inside."

"What do you think, Cassidy?" Christina asked.

Cassidy was nervous about confronting anybody about Pizzazz. *But after all, what could happen?* And Melanie was right: They might find out more by asking direct questions. She shrugged. "I guess the worst that can happen is they kick us out. Come on, let's go," she said.

The girls stepped away from the hedges and walked around the corner and into the barn.

Strangely, no one seemed to be around. There was a chair outside the horse's stall; Cassidy supposed that must be where the guard assigned to watch Pizzazz would sit. She looked around carefully, but there was no sign of Mr. Miles or the two owners she'd seen yesterday. The door of Pizzazz's stall was closed, and she didn't see the horse's head through the wire mesh that enclosed the top of the stall. *Was he lying down?*

"Where do you think the guard is?" Christina whispered, looking around.

"Maybe he went to the bathroom?" Melanie guessed.

"I guess we came at the right time," Cassidy said with a nervous giggle. "Come on, let's take a look around before someone runs us out of here." She went over to Pizzazz's stall. Christina and Melanie followed her, stepping up to the stall to peer over the top board, through the wire enclosure. Pizzazz was in the stall after all, standing with his head down, half-asleep. His front legs were soaking in buckets of ice water. A big reddish-brown chicken was busy scratching in the colt's bedding, pecking at what ever she was finding there. She kept up a throaty, croaking commentary as she scratched and pecked around the colt's feet.

"Why is there a chicken in Pizzazz's stall?" Melanie whispered.

"I don't know," Cassidy said, trying not to laugh.

"I know," Christina said. "Nervous horses some-times get a pet, like a goat, or a chicken, to calm them down. I guess this is Pizzazz's pet chicken."

"Really?" Melanie said, amazed. She looked at Cassidy for confirmation, in case Christina was teasing.

Cassidy nodded. She had seen a few racehorses in Miami who had animal companions to keep them calm, although she had never seen a racehorse with a pet chicken. "Why do you think they're soaking his legs?" Cassidy whispered, pointing to the buckets.

Christina shook her head; she didn't know.

"Is that what they do for bucked shins?" Cassidy asked.

Christina shrugged.

Cassidy's eye swept over the colt, looking for some sign that might tell her about his condition. His reddish brown tail swished slowly from side to side, occasion-ally making a rapid swat to keep off a pesky horsefly that kept landing on his flank. She took in the rise of his perfectly muscled hindquarter, the slight elegant dip of his strong back, and the red-maned slope of his neck. He was wearing a leather halter with an engraved brass nameplate, and the loop of a chain leadshank was attached to the brass ring under his chin.

Leadshank? They wouldn't leave him in the stall with a leadshank attached to his halter, Cassidy realized, unless—

Someone was in the stall with Pizzazz!

"Duck!" Cassidy hissed, putting a hand on the other girls' shoulders and ducking down herself. She peeked through a crack hoping they hadn't been noticed. All she could see were Pizzazz's legs, and a pair of worn and dirty muck boots.

But the boots were stepping toward her. The groom in the stall must have seen Cassidy at the same time she saw him. "Hey!" came a shout from inside the stall. "What are you doing there?"

9

THE CHICKEN FLEW INTO THE RAFTERS, SQUAWKING. THE horse let out a startled snort and backed into the wall. Cassidy heard a scuffle and a series of bumps, and the splash of the buckets being overturned. She cringed and turned around, ready to run out of the barn.

But when they turned, they found Mr. Miles in front of them, blocking their escape. He was standing with his hands on his hips, frowning. "What are you kids doing here?" Mr. Miles asked.

The groom pushed the stall door open and stuck his head out. He was short, not much taller than Cassidy or Christina, with thinning grayish hair. His face was flushed and angry. "Mr. Miles!" he said sharply. "These kids were snooping around here, spying. They spooked my horse!"

"We did not," Melanie exclaimed. "You spooked

him yourself, when you yelled. We were just standing there."

"We just wanted to have a look at Pizzazz," Cassidy said, trying out her most winning smile on Mr. Miles.

"We didn't mean to cause any harm," Christina added.

Mr. Miles's face relaxed. He smiled back. "Jerry, have you got the colt in hand?" he asked the groom.

"Yes, sir, he's all right," the groom said. "But—"

"Bring him out," Mr. Miles said. "You girls want to see the colt?"

"Yes, sir," Melanie said. "We're so excited about the race!" she gushed. "You're Lee Miles aren't you? I've read all about you."

Cassidy looked at her in amazement as Melanie babbled on. She really was a genius at charming her way into things.

"This morning we got to see the other horse, the filly, Lady T? And we were just dying to see Pizzazz, too! Oh, and I was wondering," Melanie said, fishing a little notebook out of the hip pocket of her jeans, "Could I have your autograph?" With a coy smile she opened the notebook to a blank page and held it out to Mr. Miles.

"Sure thing," he said amiably, taking a ballpoint pen from his chest pocket. "Now, what's your name?" he asked, pen poised over the page.

"Melissa," Melanie said. "Melissa Susan McGilli-cuddy." She beamed at him while he scribbled on the

108

pad. Cassidy had to pretend she was coughing to keep from laughing. She didn't dare look at Christina.

The groom was still looking suspiciously at them, but he had led Pizzazz out of his stall and stood holding him. Mr. Miles finished signing Melanie's book and handed it back to her. "So," he said to the girls, "what do you think of my colt?"

"Oh, he's awesome!" Cassidy said.

"Why was he standing in those buckets?" Melanie asked innocently. "Is there something wrong with his legs?"

Cassidy looked sharply at Mr. Miles, but his expression showed nothing. "No, no, this colt's legs are as good as they come," he said heartily. "We like to soak his legs after he works, just to keep down any swelling that might occur from his regular exercise. You know, sort of like a baseball pitcher icing his elbow after a game."

"Oh, I see," Melanie said. "Could we pet him?"

"Sure," Mr. Miles said. "Just pat him right here."

One by one, the girls stepped up to pat the big colt on his neck. He seemed to enjoy the attention, arching his neck and looking at them with his big curious eyes.

"I heard one of the people in the other barn say that Pizzazz stumbled the other day and that he might have hurt himself," Melanie said. "Is that true?" Her voice was full of anxious concern.

"Oh, no," Mr. Miles assured them. "Everybody likes to spread rumors. I wouldn't pay attention to any talk like that. He did stumble in a workout, but it was just a bad step. We had the vet check him out, just to be sure, and everything is fine. This horse is worth a lot of money, believe me, and he's getting the best of care."

"How was his workout this morning?" Cassidy thought to ask. Melanie shot her a keen, appreciative look.

"Par for the course," Mr. Miles said with a smile. "Now, if you girls don't mind?" He began shepherding the girls toward the barn door, while the groom led Pizzazz back into the stall. "This youngster needs his peace and quiet. He's got a big race to get ready for."

The girls thanked him and headed outside. They walked nonchalantly until they were well out of earshot of the stables, then they began talking about what they'd seen and heard.

"He's bound to have something wrong," Melanie said. "They were soaking his legs in buckets of ice water."

"Yeah, but it was both his legs," Cassidy pointed out. "It seems more likely that he'd have injured one leg, don't you think?"

"That was good thinking to ask about this morning's workout, Cassidy," Melanie said.

"Oh, right," Christina said. "That was weird, wasn't it? Why do you think he lied about it?"

"He must be trying to cover up something," Cassidy said.

"Maybe he didn't lie," Christina said. "Maybe he

just worked really early and we missed it."

Melanie shook her head. "The track was freshly harrowed when we came down, remember? We would have seen hoofprints if he worked this morning."

"True," Christina said.

"I say we tell Aunt Ashleigh what we know," Melanie said.

"Good idea," Cassidy agreed.

"And while we're at it, can we get some breakfast?" Christina asked.

"I could eat," Melanie said.

Cassidy didn't think she could eat if she tried. The whole situation bothered her. *Mr. Miles seemed so nice, but why did he lie about Pizzazz's workout?* She hoped Christina's mom would be able to tell them.

"Come on, Melissa Sue," Christina said, and giggling, the three girls ran to the house.

Over Ashleigh's famous homemade whole-wheat blueberry muffins, they sat around the big kitchen table discussing everything they knew about Pizzazz. Ashleigh listened carefully, without commenting, to the whole story.

"So what do you think, Mom?" Christina asked. "Doesn't it sound like there's something fishy going on?"

"Well," Ashleigh said, "I can see why you might be concerned. But here's what I think: The incident involving the owners and the veterinarian doesn't necessarily mean the horse isn't fit to run. There's probably a lot more to that situation than we'll ever know."

"But what about the buckets of ice water?" Melanie asked.

"What Mr. Miles said is true," Ashleigh said. "It's really not that uncommon to soak or cold-hose a performance horse's legs. And the fact that they were soaking both legs tends to make me think it really is just preventive. If he were lame, it would likely be in one leg, not both."

"That's what we thought," Cassidy said. "But then why did Mr. Miles lie about the workout? We know Pizzazz didn't work. We got down to the track before everybody."

"I don't know," Ashleigh said. "That is a little strange. But you know, he's a busy guy. Maybe he just wasn't really paying attention to the question. Or maybe they just handwalked Pizzazz this morning, and he was referring to that."

"I have a question," Cassidy said. "When I heard the owners and the vet arguing yesterday, I heard them say something like, 'Let's give him something.' And the vet said if they gave him something that the horse should be rested. Do you think they talking about drugs?" Cassidy asked.

Ashleigh frowned. "Well, yes, probably. There are some drugs that are allowed—bute, for instance. As you probably know, bute is like horse aspirin; it just eases stiff, sore muscles. The drugs that aren't allowed are certain kinds of steroids. They're 'masking' drugs. They can relieve pain if you inject them directly into a sore joint, for instance, but a horse on that kind of medication should rest. Pain is a body's signal that something is wrong. A horse in pain won't run well, although plenty of horses will try, because they have so much heart. If you use drugs to cover up the pain, the horse might run fine, but he'd be doing damage to the joint."

"Would those drugs show up when the track stewards test a horse for drugs after he runs?" Cassidy asked.

"Many don't," Ashleigh said. "That's the problem. But in my opinion, anybody who would run a horse under those circumstances ought to be in jail. A reputable trainer would never 'fix' a horse for one or a couple of races, and risk damaging him permanently."

"But what if that's what they're doing with Pizzazz?" Melanie asked.

Cassidy was thinking the same thing. She put down her muffin. It was delicious, but she was beginning to get that queasy, anxious feeling again. When she tried to decide if it was from the thought of her father losing Lady T, or the thought of Pizzazz running his heart out on an injured knee, she wasn't sure.

Ashleigh shook her head. "Honey, I know some of this stuff looks a little weird to you, but training racehorses—especially exceptional horses like Pizzazz—is a complicated business. I've known Lee Miles for years, and I simply can't believe he would ever compromise the health of a horse like Pizzazz. If it'll make you all feel any better, I'll talk to him myself. But I'm sure everything will be just fine. Don't worry."

Don't worry. How was she supposed to keep from worrying? Cassidy wondered. So many important things hinged on the match race. If the race went off as scheduled, Lady T would win. She was bound to. And even if Lady T didn't win, all she had to do was run the race, and it would still mean a lot of money—enough to help her family for a while. But what if something was really wrong with Pizzazz? If Cassidy knew about it and didn't say anything, and the horse got hurt, it would all be her fault. Whether Lady T won or lost, it would be horrible if Pizzazz broke down.

Cassidy wasn't satisfied with Ashleigh's explanation. She was becoming more and more certain that something wasn't right. But what? She had to find out.

Ashleigh excused herself to go check on something at the barn office. Christina glanced at her watch. "Hey, it's nine o'clock already. We should start getting ready to go over to Mona's."

"Before we go to Mona's, I want to try something," Cassidy said. "But I'll need your help."

"What?" Melanie asked, instantly curious.

"I want to look at Pizzazz's legs myself, up close," Cassidy said.

"Cassidy, you heard what my mom said," Christina protested. "There's probably nothing going on. Besides, we're lucky we didn't get in trouble this morning. If we

114

try snooping around again, our luck is bound to run out. I think we should just forget about it. Anyway, I thought you were so worried about losing your horse. Don't you want the race to happen?"

"Not if it means hurting a horse," Cassidy said quietly. "I've got to find out for sure what's wrong with him. Now are you guys going to help me or not?"

"I'll help you," Melanie said. "As long as I don't have to do anything illegal."

Christina sighed. "All right. But I'm with Melanie. You can't do anything that will make us get in trouble, okay?"

"You won't," Cassidy promised, getting up from the table. "I'll do all the dirty work. Let's go."

They headed out the door and followed the path that led up to the barns. There was less activity now that it was later in the morning. A few horses were still being bathed or grazed by grooms while they dried in the warm sunshine, but most of the work had been done earlier in the morning.

They were approaching the barn where Pizzazz was stabled. "How are you going to get close enough to Pizzazz to get a look at him?" Christina was saying. "I seriously doubt that Jerry guy is going to let us anywhere near the horse."

"I have a plan," Cassidy said. "This way." She led them around to the back side of the barn. There was another parking lot back there, but it was really for storing extra vehicles. The Reeses' four-horse trailer was parked there, as well as a camper belonging to Pizzazz's groom and exercise rider, and a bigger horse transport truck with the logo from the stables in California where Pizzazz was from.

Cassidy hesitated when she saw the camper. Jerry, the groom, lived in there, and so did the exercise rider. If they happened to come around just then or look out the window, Cassidy would be in plain sight of them. She would just have to take that chance, Cassidy decided.

The same neat row of hedges grew along this side of the barn as well. With a glance around to make sure no one was watching, Cassidy slipped behind the hedge, gesturing for Christina and Melanie to follow.

Bending down, the girls scurried along the wall behind the hedges until they were at the end where Pizzazz was stabled. There Cassidy stopped.

"What are you going to do?" Christina said.

"Ssh," Cassidy cautioned her, putting a finger to her lips. Slowly Cassidy stood up and peered over the windowsill into Pizzazz's stall. The horse was there alone, calmly munching his hay. Cassidy crouched down again.

"Okay, here's the plan," she whispered. "You guys boost me up, and I'll climb through the window. I'm just going to try and get a close look at Pizzazz's legs."

Melanie and Christina nodded. They got on their hands and knees under the window, and Cassidy stood up on their backs.

"Uh!" Melanie grunted.

"Gee, you're heavy," Christina complained.

"Sorry," Cassidy whispered, trying not to giggle out loud. "Pizzazz," she said very softly to the horse. "Hey, boy."

"Will you hurry up?" Melanie hissed. "You can have a conversation with him another time."

"He's got his back to me," Cassidy explained. "I don't want to spook him when I climb in. Pizzazz," she said again, trying to get the horse to look at her. Finally the colt swung his head around. His mouth was full of hay, but when he saw Cassidy, his ears pointed toward her alertly and he stopped chewing for a moment. *Was he going to spook?*

"Hey, boy," Cassidy said. "I'm just coming in for a minute. Don't be scared, okay?"

The horse regarded her for a moment, then gave a little snort and shook his head. He seemed to be saying, "Okay, it's fine with me." Then he lowered his head to grab another mouthful of hay.

Cassidy got a knee onto the windowsill, then her other foot. She perched precariously for a moment, trying to decide what would be the best way to come down into the stall without making any noise or scaring the horse. Somehow she managed to twist around and lower herself onto the floor.

As she dropped the last couple of feet, Pizzazz's head shot up and he let out a snort. The he stomped one hind foot hard a couple of times. Cassidy froze, crouching under the window where she had landed. Luckily no one came in and, after a moment, with an impatient toss of his head, the colt settled down and began munching his hay again. Cassidy saw a big horsefly zoom over her head out the window and breathed a sigh of relief. It was the fly that had been aggravating the colt.

She waited another few seconds, to be sure no one was coming, then she moved cautiously closer to the colt. "Hey, Pizzazz," she said in a soft sweet voice that she hoped would soothe the colt. He didn't seem bothered anymore, so she crept right up to his front legs and slowly put a hand on his shoulder. "I'm just going to take a look at you for a minute, okay, big boy?" she whispered.

Suddenly Cassidy saw the outline of someone's feet right outside the stall and realized that the security guard was sitting there. *Did he hear me?* Again she froze, breathing through her mouth without making a sound, ready to bolt for the window if the feet moved. Her heart sounded so loud to her, she thought the guard surely must be able to hear it, and she placed a hand over it, willing herself to be calm. To her relief, the guard stayed where he was.

Cassidy craned her ears, listening for any sounds in the barn, but everything was quiet except for the normal sounds of barn life and content horses in their stalls. Somewhere she could hear the familiar swish of a broom on the concrete floor. She was about to go on examining Pizzazz's legs, when she heard a strange rumbling sound coming from right outside the stall. *What's that?* she thought, feeling a surge of adrenaline that started her heart pounding all over again.

It came again, a sort of low growling noise. Then she realized what it was and had to swallow a laugh. The guard was fast asleep, snoring loudly.

Quickly Cassidy began examining the Pizzazz's right foreleg, which was nearest to her. She ran both hands slowly down the horse's leg, feeling for any areas of heat, which would indicate inflammation. She looked closely for swelling in the knee and ankle, but everything looked normal as far as she could tell. There were no marks or scars on the leg. Sliding her hand down the inside of his leg she felt a rough, scaly lump, then realized it was only a "chestnut," one of the small horny growths that all horses have on their legs. Then she ran her hand down the tendon in back of his leg and picked up his foot. It was perfectly clean, as healthy-looking a hoof as she had ever seen. She set his foot down.

Cassidy stood, crouching a little so that her head wouldn't be seen over the horse's back if anyone looked in on him, and laying an arm on top of his rump so he would know she was there, moved around to his left side. Just as she stepped around him, he swished his tail hard. Cassidy got it right in the face and winced. "Ow," she whispered, rubbing at her cheek. "Thanks a lot, Pizzazz," she muttered. Her cheek still stinging from the swat, she knelt by the colt's shoulder and began to check out his left front leg.

She had been jumpy about being in the stall at first, but now she'd forgotten to be nervous. She simply concentrated on examining Pizzazz's leg. Once he switched his tail hard several times and shifted his hindquarters away from her. Cassidy paused, waiting for him to settle down again. Then she saw what was bothering him: The horsefly was back, or another one just like it. The fly landed on Pizzazz's hip. It was a big one, as big as the horsefly that had sent Sterling into a bucking frenzy in the jump class at Mona's the other day. With one expert flip of his long tail, Pizzazz got the fly. Then he went on devouring his hay.

When he was peaceful again, Christina picked up the colt's left front foot. But then she had to drop it. There was a terrible, stinging pain in her right arm. She looked and saw that the horsefly, foiled by the colt's handy tail, had landed on her arm and was biting her! She slapped at it angrily and it flew off, leaving a red mark and a trickle of blood where it had bitten her.

Cassidy picked up the colt's foot again and checked it out. Nothing. She set the hoof down. Feeling both glad and disappointed, she was just about to sneak around Pizzazz's rump again and head for the window, when she saw the fly land on the inside of the colt's right foreleg. She stopped, waiting for him to get rid of the fly. She didn't want to get kicked or stepped on. But the horse stood still.

Cassidy stared at the fly. It was huge and ugly. She shuddered and glanced at her arm, which was still bleeding from the bite. She wiped off the blood and cleaned her hand on her jeans. No wonder Sterling had gone crazy. Cassidy's bite was still smarting and beginning to itch.

The horsefly was still sitting on Pizzazz's right front leg, on the inside of his knee. It was obviously gorging itself on the colt's blood. Cassidy watched, repulsed and fascinated at the same time. Pizzazz continued to munch peacefully.

An alarm went off in Cassidy's mind. *Why isn't Pizzazz reacting to the fly? It has to hurt.* She knew how much it had hurt her own arm. *How can he stand it? Unless . . . unless he can't feel it!*

10

HORRIFIED, CASSIDY SWIPED AT THE FLY WITH HER HAND. Pizzazz wasn't reacting to the fly because he couldn't feel it biting him! A trail of blood began to ooze from the spot where the fly had been. Cassidy poked a finger at the area, watching for the colt's reaction. Nothing. Then she took a little skin and pinched it hard between her fingernails. The colt didn't move. She tried the same experiment on the other leg and had to jerk back a little when he stomped impatiently at the sharp pinch.

Then the horsefly, attracted by the blood, came back and settled on Pizzazz's knee again. Again it attached itself, and the colt made no response. Now Cassidy was sure. The colt's right front leg was numb around the area of his knee. She swatted at the horsefly again, knocking it to the ground. She moved under the colt's neck and stepped on the fly, grinding hard with her sneaker to be sure she killed it. Then she scurried to the window again, crouching low. Cassidy listened for a moment. The guard had stopped snoring, but everything was still quiet. She stood up cautiously and was about to peek out the window when suddenly there was a face in front of her!

Cassidy almost cried out. Then she realized that it was only Christina. "Hurry up and get out of there, will you?" Christina whispered urgently. "Mr. Miles is on his way into the barn!"

Cassidy nodded that she understood, and with a glance behind her to be sure no one was looking, put her hands on the windowsill and jumped up. Just as she did, there was a loud squawking and flapping from behind her. At first she was scared to death. Then she realized it was only the chicken, Pizzazz's stablemate. It must have flown down from the rafters and been startled by Cassidy as she jumped for the windowsill. But the commotion was loud; it might bring someone hurrying to check on Pizzazz. With her heart thudding and the chicken still clucking indignantly behind her, Cassidy scrambled through the window and dropped head first behind the hedge.

It would have hurt if she had fallen on the gravel that covered the ground under the hedges. But instead Cassidy fell on top of something. "Oof!" the thing said.

She realized she had landed right on top of Melanie. "Ow," Melanie said.

"Sorry," Cassidy said, giggling. "But I had to make a

quick getaway. Thanks for breaking my fall," she added.

"Thanks for squashing me flat," Melanie retorted. "Now would you mind getting off of me? I can hardly breathe."

"Sorry," Cassidy said again. She untangled herself from Melanie and got up, awkwardly. There was a big scrape on one of her arms but otherwise she was fine. She could hear the chicken still clucking loudly inside the stall. "Come on, let's get out of here before that chicken comes after me," she said. They scurried behind the hedges alongside the barn, back the way they'd come, and cautiously emerged at opposite end of the barn.

Cassidy told the girls what she'd discovered, that the horse's right leg was numb around his knee. "It makes sense, when you put it together with what I heard Pizzazz's owners talking about and what Christina's mom told us," Cassidy said. "They've got to be giving him masking drugs. Poor Pizzazz," she said.

"But I don't see what we can do about it," Christina said.

"What do you mean? When we tell them about his leg, they'll have to call off the race," Cassidy said.

"Tell who?" Melanie asked. "Who are we going to tell?"

Cassidy thought for a second, then said, "Well, Christina's mom, I guess."

"And exactly what are we going to tell her? That they should call off the match race because you thought the horse was too calm about a fly biting his leg?" Christina said. "No way. They'll never go for it."

"Yeah, you know how grownups are," Melanie said. "First of all, they'd never believe you about the fly. Even though we do," she added quickly. "And second of all, even if they did, Christina's right. It's not exactly enough evidence to call off the whole race."

Slowly it began to dawn on Cassidy. They were right. Even if they got anyone to believe the story about the fly, it didn't guarantee they would stop the race. Probably, she'd just get in trouble for being in Pizzazz's stall.

"I think it's time to quit worrying about Pizzazz," Christina said. "I bet he'll be just fine. And even if he isn't one-hundred-percent okay, it's like my mom said. They wouldn't risk injuring such a valuable horse for one race."

"I guess you're right," Cassidy said. "It just seems like there ought to be something we could do." She sighed.

"You've done everything you can," Melanie said.

Cassidy reluctantly agreed. She really had tried. Melanie and Christina were right; the race would probably go on no matter what she did. She had to admit, she didn't really want to be responsible for stopping the race. It was a relief to know that her dad would be able to keep Lady T and would get some money from the race. *But had she really done everything she could?* Deep inside, Cassidy wasn't so sure.

125

The rest of the day, Cassidy tried to forget about Pizzazz and the race and everything else that had been troubling her. She loved Saturdays at Mona's, because she could take her time with both her horses. She exercised Rebound, no jumping, just a light hack. Then she spent an hour grooming him, brushing his sleek, dark coat until it seemed to shine with a light of its own. When she reached an especially itchy spot on the inside of his thigh, he leaned into the currycomb, groaning happily.

Cassidy laughed. "You like that, huh? How about this side?" She walked around his rear and began rubbing the same spot on the other side. Rebound enjoyed it just as much. When she couldn't possibly have gotten one more speck of dirt off him anywhere, she unclipped the crossties and led him back into his stall. He didn't go right for his hay. Instead he turned to face her, looking at her alertly with his big, dark eyes. Cassidy had been about to close the stall door but she couldn't resist going back to give him one more pat. Rebound nuzzled her arm gently with his soft lips. Cassidy leaned against her horse, her arms encircling his neck, and rested her head against him for a moment.

"I love you so much," Cassidy murmured. "What would I ever do without you?" She realized then that, as hard as the move had been on her and her family, at least she still had her horses. Whatever else she had to deal with, she knew she would manage somehow as long as she had Rebound and Wellington.

When she had finished with Rebound, Cassidy noticed that Wellington's mane was getting too long and shaggy, so she spent an hour pulling it short and thin. When she finished, she stepped back to eye it. Then she put down the pulling comb, satisfied with the job she had done. She was just finishing grooming him when she heard Melanie's voice.

"Hey, Cassidy, want to go on the trails with me and Christina?"

Cassidy looked up and saw Melanie standing just outside the barn holding Trib. She had been planning to school Welly in the ring, but a trail ride sounded like a great idea. "Sure, be right there," she called, and went to get Wellington's bridle.

Some days Cassidy loved the serious training she had to put in with her horses in order to be competitive in horse shows. But lately she'd really been enjoying just bumming around the pasture, taking it easy. At the barn in Miami there hadn't been any trails; she could only ride in the arenas.

She slipped the bit in Wellington's mouth and positioned the bridle on his head, buckling up the throatlatch to secure it. She started to put the saddle on him, then decided to ride bareback instead. She zipped her chaps on over her shorts, fastened her helmet, and led Wellington outside where there was a big boulder she could use for a mounting block.

"How was your lesson?" she asked Christina, who was waiting outside with Melanie.

"Great!" Christina said. "I used to think flatwork was so boring, but I have to say, it sure seems to help Sterling."

"I know what you mean," Cassidy said. "I always think I'd rather just be jumping, but whenever I have a flat lesson, it always makes the jumping so much better." She stepped up on the boulder and scrambled up on Wellington's broad back. "Okay, let's go." She gathered up the reins and headed out toward the back pasture behind Sterling and Trib.

The girls spent a blissful hour ambling along the trails that ran all over Mona's land, up and down hills, through woods and open fields. Cassidy was as completely happy as she had ever been, until they came up over the crest of a hill where Mona's land backed Whitebrook. Then she got a glimpse of the white fenced training oval and that reminded her of the race all over again. She got a sort of queasy feeling in her stomach when she pictured Lady T and Pizzazz running against each other. It made her want to forget about horses for a while.

"I think I'm ready to head back," she told the other two girls.

"I guess we should be getting home, too," Christina said.

"See you tomorrow?" Cassidy asked.

"Sure," Melanie said.

"See you tomorrow," Christina agreed. She and Melanie walked on over the crest of the hill in the direction of the fence that separated Gardener Farm from Whitebrook. Cassidy waved at them, then headed back toward Mona's barn, wishing for the first time that she didn't know so much about horses.

The match race was set for the following Saturday. The days before the race seemed to creep by, each one slower than the one before. "I thought the days were supposed to be getting shorter," Cassidy complained to Melanie in the school cafeteria on Thursday. Her tray sat before her; she had barely touched the food, and for a change it wasn't too bad—lasagna. She had spent the week alternating between being totally excited about the race and being overcome with worry about Pizzazz.

Melanie shook her head. "It's one of those weird laws of nature. The more anxious you are for it to be a certain day, the longer it takes before you get to that day. It's like Christmas," she suggested. "You know how you think it'll never come?"

Cassidy gave her an amused look. "I know what you mean," she agreed. "Except that mostly you want Christmas to come. I'm not sure if I want Saturday to come or not," she said grimly.

"You're not still worrying about Pizzazz, are you?" Melanie asked.

Cassidy nodded. "I just can't help it. I know what I

saw, and I know it doesn't sound like much, but I just have a bad feeling about it." She put down her fork and pushed her tray back a few inches so she could rest her forearms on the table. "If only I could have talked to that vet," she said with a sigh.

"Mind if we join you?"

Cassidy looked up to see who had spoken and smiled when she saw Dylan standing over her with his tray. She scooted over to make room for him, and he plopped his tray down and sat beside her.

"Hey, Mel," he said, leaning back to speak to Melanie who was sitting on Cassidy's other side.

"Hey, Dyl," Melanie said.

A moment later Kevin came over and sat down across from Melanie. "Hey, guys," he said.

"So do you mind if I ask what's been bugging you all week?" Dylan said to Cassidy, taking a bite of lasagna.

"She's freaked out about the match race," Melanie told him.

"Why?" Kevin asked.

Cassidy told the boys everything that had happened, starting with seeing Pizzazz stumble. "I know I should just forget about it; it's probably nothing," she said. "But I just can't get it out of my head. I wish there was some way I could talk to the vet about what I overheard that day," she said.

"Well, what's his name?" Dylan asked.

"I don't know," Cassidy said. "I never heard them

say. They just kept calling him 'Doc.' And once I heard Mr. Miles call him Sam."

"Doc Sam," Dylan said. "Hmm. Not much you can do with that." He thought for a moment. "Hasn't been back to the barn since then?"

Cassidy shook her head. "I'm pretty sure he won't be coming around again. Especially after the way that guy grabbed him and threatened to punch him."

"And you can't exactly go around asking the guy's name. That would definitely make them suspicious," Kevin said thoughtfully. "Can you think of anything else you might have noticed about the guy?"

Cassidy thought about it. "Well, I know what he looked like," she said.

"Would you recognize him if you saw him?" Melanie asked.

Cassidy nodded. "I'm pretty sure I would. And I think I would recognize his voice. And I know what his truck looked like, because I saw him drive away." She described his truck.

"Did you happen to get his license plate number?" Kevin asked.

Cassidy frowned, trying to remember. "I know it was from California," she said. "But I'm not sure about the actual license number. I think it was mostly letters, and it started with a D. But I can't remember the whole thing."

"Too bad," Kevin said. "You know, if you know somebody's license plate number, you can find out lots

131

of stuff about them. I learned that from this book I've been reading about how the FBI investigates stuff. It's fascinating. I'm thinking about becoming a private investigator."

"Really?" Melanie said, sounding impressed.

"Yep," Kevin said. "You can make tons of money doing really big secret jobs. And you get to travel all over the place if you're following somebody. It's totally cool."

"I sure wish you could find that vet for me," Cassidy said. "If only I could talk to him. He's the one who would really know what's wrong with Pizzazz and whether or not he should run."

"But don't you want the race to happen?" Dylan asked. "I mean, your dad's going to get a ton of money even if Lady T loses. And if Pizzazz does have some kind of injury, it can't be that serious, or they wouldn't be running him, right? Maybe it'll just slow him down."

"That's what everybody keeps telling me," Cassidy said. "But I still wish I could talk to the vet. I'd feel a whole lot better if he could tell me that Pizzazz was really okay to run.

That night at dinner, Cassidy decided to tell her parents what she knew about Pizzazz. Her father listened to the story, then put down his fork and looked seriously at her. "Cassidy, listen," he said. "I know this sounds like something strange is going on, but the most likely reason for the vet stomping off the way you described is that he had some kind of disagreement with the owners—probably about money."

"But Dad," she said, "wouldn't you feel better about the race if you knew Pizzazz was one-hundred-percent okay? I mean, you wouldn't want to risk him being injured, would you?" she asked.

"Who are you, the teenaged racing commissioner?" Campbell said sarcastically. "There's nothing wrong with that horse. Don't you know he's worth like a million dollars? They're not going to run him if he's lame."

Money, Cassidy thought. *Why does everything always have to be about money?* "They might," she retorted. "What if he's got some kind of condition that's not going to get any better, so this is his last race?"

"Cassidy, that's so unlikely," her mother, Leslie Smith, said. She smiled at Cassidy. "Honey, try not to get so worked up about this. I know how involved you get with your horses, but—"

"Mom, this isn't about my horses," Cassidy pointed out. "It's about Pizzazz."

"Aren't you excited about the race?" Cassidy's father said. "Don't you know how important this race is for Lady T's career?"

"And for your dad's?" Leslie said softly. "The race money will really help, even if Lady T doesn't win. In one more month he can start training again, but right now things are a little tight for us."

Campbell snorted. "A little?"

"That'll do, Campbell," Harrison Smith said. "The point is, things have been tough since the move and all the controversy in Miami, but we're over the worst of it. This race is going to get us back on our feet." He smiled at his family and raised his glass of iced tea. "Here's to the match race. May this be the best Saturday of our lives."

Leslie Smith smiled back at her husband and raised her own glass. Even Campbell, who never liked to participate in family rituals, raised his glass. Cassidy reluctantly joined in, clinking her water glass against theirs and taking a sip. She was still full of doubt, but she guessed her dad was probably right. And it was the first time in months that he had sounded so happy.

Cassidy was sitting in the grandstand at a huge race track. Spectators were all around her, many using binoculars to see across to the far side of the track. To Cassidy, who didn't have any, the track looked as vast as an ocean. "Where are they? Can you see them?" she asked a woman standing next to her.

The woman turned to Cassidy, without taking down the binoculars she held to her eyes. Cassidy recognized the woman's strawberry-blond hair. It was Ashleigh. "There's no way to tell," Ashleigh said. "Here, see for yourself."

Ashleigh handed Cassidy the binoculars. She aimed them out toward the vast race track, but instead of a pack of horses speeding around the track, Cassidy saw her father and a tall, gray-haired man wearing wire-rimmed glasses—a veterinarian. Her father was holding a reddish-brown chicken. "Here, Cassidy," he said, "She was supposed to be in the race. You take her."

Cassidy reached for the chicken, which seemed to be hurt somehow . . . her wing? But Cassidy was so far away, her arms wouldn't reach. "Dad, come closer," she said. "I can't reach her."

The vet looked at her gravely. "Then I'm afraid the chicken will have to be put down," he said. He got in his truck and drove away.

"Wait," Cassidy said. "I'll try again." She reached as hard as she could, and it seemed like her arms might stretch long enough. But her father was too far away. Cassidy gave the binoculars back to Ashleigh. "I can't use these," she said.

"Try the other end," Ashleigh said. Cassidy turned the binoculars around and peered through the wide end. Now she could see the back of the vet's truck through the double circles of the binocular lenses. DRSFINE, the license plate said. "That's funny," Cassidy said. "I thought I wouldn't remember those letters." She put the binoculars down and looked around.

Everything was dark. With a jolt, Cassidy realized that she had been dreaming. She lay still for a moment, struggling to bring the dream to her consciousness.

Slowly bits of it came to her; she had thought she was at the races. She almost laughed aloud, remembering the chicken that was supposed to race the horses. Then she recalled the end of the dream and bolted upright in her bed, every muscle in her body tense with excitement.

11

"DRSFINE," CASSIDY SAID ALOUD. "DRSFINE, DRS-FINE," she repeated rapidly. "D-R—Doctor," she said. Doctor Sfine? Doc. Sam. Suddenly it came to her. "Sam! Doctor S. Fine—Doctor Sam Fine!"

Cassidy threw the covers off and swung her legs around to the floor. She checked the clock. Twelve-twenty. It would be ten-twenty in California. Late, but not too late. She got up and tiptoed into the kitchen. Silently she lifted the cordless phone from its base and dialed long distance information. "What city?" the operator asked.

For a second, Cassidy wasn't sure what to say. She couldn't just ask for any Dr. Sam Fine. California was a huge state. There could be fifty of them. Then she remembered. Pizzazz was stabled at Santa Anita Park. "Um . . . Santa Anita?" she said, talking quietly so she wouldn't wake her brother or her parents.

"What listing?"

"Doctor Sam Fine," she said. She grabbed a pen and a notepad from the kitchen counter and waited.

"I have no listing for Doctor Sam Fine in Santa Anita. Would you like me to try Arcadia?"

"Oh . . . yes, please," Cassidy said. Arcadia? She guessed it must be near Santa Anita.

"One moment . . ."

There was a click and the recorded message came on, "The number you have requested, area code eight, one, eight . . . five, seven, four . . ." Carefully Cassidy took down the whole number. She hoped it was the right Dr. Fine. She hung up. Then she took a deep breath and dialed the number.

Two rings. "Dr. Fine," said the voice at the end of the line. To Cassidy's relief, it sounded like the voice of the vet. And he sounded wide awake.

"Hello, Dr. Fine? I'm sorry to disturb you, but . . ." Cassidy paused, trying to decide exactly how to explain herself.

"Yes? What's the trouble?" His voice was calm.

"I'm . . . I want to ask you about a horse," Cassidy said.

"Your horse is sick?" Dr. Fine said. "What's the matter with him?"

"No, he's not sick, exactly," Cassidy said. "Not my horse."

"Then what's the trouble? You sound mighty

138

young," he said suspiciously. "Is this a prank? I don't have time for this nonsense. If you're playing around on the phone, I'll make sure you get in trouble."

"It's not a prank," Cassidy said quickly. "Please listen to me. I want to ask you about Pizzazz."

"Pizzazz?" the vet said. "Who is this?"

Cassidy hesitated. *Should I tell him my name?* Then she decided it would be okay. After all, she knew his name. "My name is Cassidy Smith," she said. "I'm calling from Kentucky."

"Kentucky? Do your parents know you're up making long-distance calls?"

Cassidy ignored that question. "I was at Whitebrook, the day you left," she said. "I heard you tell the owners of Pizzazz that he wasn't fit to run. I know you're right because I've been watching the horse. I know he can't feel anything in his right knee, but I don't know what's wrong with him. Will you tell me what it is? If you do, maybe I can get someone to believe me and stop the race."

There was a long pause at the end of the line. Then Dr. Fine said, "Are you a reporter?"

Cassidy was puzzled. A reporter? "No," she said. "I'm just a kid."

Dr. Fine laughed. "A kid, huh? Well, listen, kid. What's your name? Cassidy?"

"Yes," Cassidy said.

"I don't know why I'm telling you this, except I care for the horse, and I'd like him to have a life," the vet

139

said. "Listen carefully. Pizzazz has a bone chip in his knee, and it's started to cause problems. When he puts stress on the joint, as he does during a workout, the bone chip rubs on the cartilage in his knee. It hurts. So they give him a drug to numb the knee, and then he doesn't feel any pain. So he keeps on running. But while he's running, that bone chip is in there, chewing up the cartilage in his knee. The horse doesn't feel it; he feels fine, because the drug is masking the pain. But pretty soon the cartilage will be torn to shreds."

"That's awful," Cassidy said softly. "Isn't there anything they can do for him?"

"That's the worst part," Dr. Fine said. "There is something they could do. They could stop running him and do arthroscopic surgery to remove the bone chip. Then when the cartilage heals, his knee will be in good shape again. He'll probably have a long and successful career. But they don't want to do the surgery until after he runs that crazy match race tomorrow."

"Will he be able to run?" Cassidy asked.

"Sure, with what they're giving him, he'll run all right. He might make it. He might even win. But it'll likely be the last time he ever runs."

Cassidy felt a chill run through her. The idea of making a horse run under those conditions was appalling. "Is . . . is that all?" Cassidy asked.

"That's pretty much it, in a nutshell," the vet said.

"Can't you say something?" Cassidy asked.

"I did," the vet said. "I quit as the horse's vet. But I

can't go around saying that the owners and the trainers are jeopardizing the horse, because the truth is, he might make it one more race. I sincerely hope he does, though in my opinion it's not likely. But they'll get somebody else, some other vet, to say he's okay. I'm sure they already have. So it'd just be my word against theirs. And anyway, fifty million people are waiting to see this race. It's a big media event. And it's tomorrow. They're not going to call it off now, no matter what I say or who I talk to. Good luck, kid. I hope you can find some way to get them to stop the race. But don't get your hopes up."

"I'm sure going to try," Cassidy promised. She thanked him and hung up the phone, her heart racing. She had been right all along. *Pizzazz did have an injury!* The vet had told her all about it. Now they would have to believe her.

"Cassidy?" someone said, and the kitchen light came on, nearly blinding her.

"Dad!" Cassidy said. "Listen, I have to tell you something."

"What are you doing up at this hour?" His blond hair was tousled, and his eyes were bleary. "It's nearly one o'clock in the morning. Were you on the phone?"

"Dad, listen," Cassidy said urgently. She went over and took his hand, leading him to the kitchen table. He reluctantly pulled out a chair and sat down. "I was just talking to Dr. Fine, Pizzazz's vet. I mean, he used to be Pizzazz's vet," Cassidy corrected herself. She told her father what she knew about the horse's condition. "So we have to call off the race. Even if no one else will believe me, I know you will. You own Lady T. So you can call off the race and save Pizzazz."

Harrison Smith was looking at his daughter with an older version of her green eyes. He was slowly shaking his head. "Cassidy, we can't," he said. "We can't call off the race."

"What are you talking about?" Cassidy said. "Weren't you listening to me? If he races, Pizzazz's knee might be torn to shreds! Dr. Fine said. We have to stop that race!"

"We can't," Harrison Smith said simply. "I can't."

Cassidy stared at him. "Dad! What do you mean?"

He sighed. "Cassidy, there's so much more to all this than you know," he said. "It's complicated. We can't just cancel the race."

"Why not?" she said.

Harrison Smith rubbed his eyes with his fingertips. Then he ran his hands over his thick, blond hair in a distracted sort of way. Cassidy had the feeling she was seeing some other part of her father that she'd never seen before. Feeling uneasy, she waited.

Finally, he spoke. "You know the suspension hit me hard," he said.

Cassidy nodded. She knew he was talking about having his trainer's license suspended.

"You know since the move, your mom and I have been having some financial problems." He looked at her to be sure she understood.

142

"I know," she said quietly. "I've heard you and Mom talking."

Cassidy's dad reached across the table and took one of her hands in both of his. "Honey, I hope it doesn't come to this, I really do. . . ." He paused and stared at Cassidy's hand, searching for words. Cassidy looked at him intently. She had no idea why, but suddenly she was afraid of what he was going to say.

"The fact is," he went on, still looking at her hand. "We're having a tough time meeting all the expenses right now. When I lost my license . . ." he trailed off for a moment and Cassidy saw a look of sadness and resignation flash across his face before he continued.

"It's like this, Cassidy," he said. "Lady T is the only thing part of my career that I still have. And until my suspension is lifted, I had to make a deal with a couple of guys, just so I could afford to keep her in training and keep her racing. She's got to run this match race. Even if she loses, my cut will be enough to pay them back the money I owe them. But if she doesn't race, I'm going to lose her, Cassidy. Do you understand?" He looked up at her, squeezing her hand hard. His voice was low and intense. "Win or lose, she has to run this race. She has to run. Because if she doesn't, I'll lose her. And she's all I have left. Cassidy, if we lose Lady T . . ." He paused again and looked at her helplessly. "I don't know how to say this, but we won't be able to afford to keep your horses anymore. If this race doesn't happen, we'll have to sell Rebound and Wellington."

143

Cassidy stared at her father, speechless. *Could this be true? Would he really sell Rebound and Wellington?* Cassidy could hardly listen to the rest of what he was saying. She felt numb. He was mumbling something about the race tomorrow, about the track veterinarian.

"... when the track vet examines him, he'll know if there's anything wrong with the colt," he was saying, in a tone that Cassidy assumed was meant to reassure her. It was the same voice he'd used to soothe her when she was little and had had a bad dream. But she wasn't little anymore. And this wasn't a dream. "And if the track vet okays him, then it's fine. He can run."

"Dad," Cassidy said. "You know that's not true. There are masking drugs. They keep the horse feeling good, even though he might really be injured."

"How do you know about masking drugs?" he said, frowning.

"I know about lots of things," Cassidy said softly. She met her father's gaze unwaveringly. "I know that some drugs won't show up when the track vet examines the horse. Or after the race, when they test for drugs. If he can still walk after the race," she said coldly.

"Cassidy, that's not necessarily true," he protested. "Sometimes trainers do give certain substances to their horses, but it's to help them, not to hurt them."

"Drugs are illegal, Dad," Cassidy said.

He sighed. "You have no idea what you're talking about, Cassidy. Training top racehorses is a completely different world from the hunters and jumpers you have

144

experience with. People in my business are faced with a lot of pressure to turn out winning animals. And there are lots of substances out there that really do help horses with problems. I used them myself early in my career," he said gently.

"Illegal drugs?" Cassidy was completely shocked. "How could you?" she said, stunned.

"It was a long time ago, Cass, before I realized I didn't have to do everything the owners were telling me to do. And that wasn't the case this last time in Florida. I know better now."

"Then you agree with me," Cassidy said. "If a horse is hurt, he shouldn't run. Somebody should say 'no.' They shouldn't let him run and mask his pain with drugs, right?"

Her father shook his head. "It's a lot more complicated than that, Cassidy."

"But Pizzazz could really get hurt, Dad. You have to call off the race, please."

"I'm afraid I can't do that, honey. We don't know the whole story. You want to keep your horses, don't you?" he said quietly.

Cassidy thought about Rebound, her gentle, spirited jumper. She thought about all the big horse shows she'd taken him to when she lived in Miami and everything was still okay. And Wellington, with his beautiful, smooth trot and his unbelievable canter. Welly, who could be so perfect in the hunter ring and then suddenly let out a huge buck, because he was still young and playful. Cassidy almost smiled thinking of him. Then just as quickly tears began to blur her eyes as she thought what it would mean to lose them both. Slowly she stood up from the table. Biting her lip ferociously to keep from sobbing out loud, she turned without a word and went to her room.

Saturday morning Cassidy's father acted completely normal. It was as though the whole scene the night before had never taken place.

They were all going to the match race of course. Her parents were excited about the race and even Campbell was going. It was supposed to be "the big day."

Cassidy felt terrible. She almost stayed at home, but then she decided to go. If she stayed home, there was nothing she could do except wait for the outcome of the race. If she went to the track she might still find some way to help Pizzazz.

Keeneland was only about a twenty-minute drive from the Smiths' house. Cassidy sat in the backseat, staring out the window. Her father had given them each a paddock pass, a laminated card on a metal ball chain. Cassidy hung hers around her neck.

At the track, Cassidy peeled off the sticker from her ticket stub and stuck it on her shirt. "I'm going to check out the paddock area," she informed her parents.

"Cassidy, wait," her mom said. "I don't think you should be going by yours—"

Cassidy heard her mom, but she pretended not to. She quickly disappeared in the crowd. Once on her own, she headed for the holding barns behind the paddock area. She had agreed to meet Christina and Melanie back there.

"Hi!" she said, spotting Melanie. "Oh, nice hair!" she said, noting Melanie's new shade of Kool-aid blue.

"Thanks," Melanie said, with a toss of her bright-blue bangs. "I did it especially for the match race." Grinning, she leaned over and whispered in Cassidy's ear, "Christina hates it! She's, like, so embarrassed."

Cassidy laughed. "It looks good on you. Where is Christina anyway?" she asked, looking around.

"She went to find a bathroom," Melanie said.

Just then Christina came walking up the shedrow. "Hi, Cassidy," she said with a wave.

"Hey, Christina," Cassidy said.

"Where are your folks?" Christina asked.

"I ditched them, what do you think?" Cassidy said.

"We did, too," Melanie said. "Who wants to hang around with grownups?" she made a face, wrinkling her nose.

"So, you want to go check out the competition?" Christina asked the other girls.

"Do we have time?" Cassidy asked.

"Sure," Christina said. "The match race is sixth. Do you want to watch the other races?"

Cassidy shook her head. "I don't really care about the

other races. I want to check on Pizzazz, but first I want to go visit Lady T. Do you have any idea where she is?"

"Yep," Melanie said. "We already staked out the place. Right this way." She started down the shedrow.

Cassidy and Christina followed. Melanie led them to a stall in the holding barn, where horses were boarded who trailered in, instead of living at the track. "There she is," Melanie pointed.

Lady T stood sedately in her stall, her beautiful head hanging over the stall guard, looking with a disdainful curiosity up and down the aisle. Charlie McGowan sat on a chair outside her stall.

"Hi, Charlie," Melanie called.

"Hey, girls," he said agreeably. "Ready for the big race?"

"I guess so," Melanie said. "You still betting on Lady T, Charlie?"

"Yep!" Charlie patted his breast pocket. "Already got my winning ticket."

Cassidy went over to the filly and patted her sleek neck. She looked at Cassidy almost politely, then swung her head around to watch another horse being led in after his bath.

"Listen, don't let Frank see you petting her, okay, Missy?" Charlie said. "I don't care, but he's particular, especially on race days. You understand?"

"Sure, Charlie," Cassidy said. She didn't see why he should care if she patted the horse. After all, the filly did belong to her father.

"Cassidy's dad owns her," Melanie said. "She should be able to pet Lady T anytime she wants to."

"Sweetheart, if it were up to me, she could sleep in the stall with that horse if that's what she wanted. All of you could, for that matter. But the fact is, the trainer's the boss, and I have to do what he tells me. There have already been dozens of reporters around here this morning, trying to get a picture, or an interview, or whatever." He chuckled. "They keep coming around, asking to see her. And Frank keeps sending them over there." He pointed.

Cassidy looked. The horse he was pointing to was a few stalls down. "But that's not Lady T," Cassidy said.

"You know that, and I know that, but believe it or not, most people can't tell the difference," Charlie said.

"You're kidding," Christina said.

Cassidy looked carefully at the other horse. It was about the same size as Lady T and the same color. But that was it as far as the similarities went.

Melanie went over to get a closer look. "I can't believe they think this is Lady T!" she exclaimed. Then she looked closer and began to laugh. "This isn't even a filly! It's a gelding!"

Charlie shared a good laugh with the girls. Then he said, "Even if they didn't know that, you'd think they'd read the name plate on the halter."

Sure enough, both the gelding and Lady T wore leather halters with brass name plates. "Boy, it's hard to believe people can be fooled that easily," Cassidy said.

Charlie shrugged. "People just see what they want to see, I guess," he said.

"But why don't they want anyone to take Lady T's picture?" Melanie asked.

"She's got a big race today," Charlie said. "The trainer wants her left alone."

"But look, Charlie, she doesn't want to be left alone," Christina said. "She likes the company."

It seemed true. The filly was eagerly eyeing every horse or person who made a sound.

"She's a little worked up today, that's a fact," Charlie said. "That filly's usually as aloof as a cat. I never saw so her act so social."

"She knows she's got a big job to do today, don't you, pretty girl?" Melanie said, going over to stand by the filly.

"You know, I think you're right. I could swear they know when it's race day," Charlie observed. "The track vet was just here to examine her, and she started fussing the minute he set foot in the barn. It's like she knew he was going to poke at her."

"The track vet?" Cassidy asked. "Where was he going next?"

"Over to the other side," Charlie motioned behind the filly. "To examine the colt."

Cassidy turned to Melanie and Christina. "Let's go," she said.

"We'll come with you," Christina said.

The three girls hurried down the shedrow and

turned left. On this side of the barn another row of stalls with its own shedrow backed the other row. Right away Cassidy spotted Pizzazz. He stood in the shedrow while the track veterinarian did the pre-race exam to ensure that he was fit to run.

Maybe he won't pass, Cassidy thought, as she approached. *Maybe they'll find something in his knee.*

A group of photographers was gathered around, snapping pre-race photos. Mr. Miles was giving an interview to a crew with a television camera. Cassidy watched hopefully as the vet finished the exam. Smiling for the cameras, the vet signed the approval papers and gave the "thumbs-up" sign. Pizzazz was going to race.

Cassidy turned away. She couldn't look at the horse. "I don't understand," she said. "How could the vet okay him? He's a doctor. He ought to be able to tell there's something wrong with the horse's knee."

"Cassidy, get over it, will you? Apparently there isn't anything wrong with him," Christina said. "Aren't you glad, for heaven's sake?"

Cassidy shook her head. Then she told Christina and Melanie about her midnight conversation with Dr. Fine. "So the horse is running with a damaged knee, and everybody but me seems to think it's perfectly all right," Cassidy said. "Even my father. I can't believe it." She didn't mention what he'd said about selling her horses. Every time she thought about it she got all choked up. She didn't trust herself to talk about it without crying.

They had been walking out back, behind the receiving barns, wandering in and out between the campers and cars and trucks belonging to the staff of various barns. Suddenly Cassidy saw a horse being led toward a small transport truck by a groom, with another following behind, looking around as if he were alert for some kind of trouble. One of the grooms looked familiar; Cassidy recognized him. It was Jerry, the groom she had seen with Pizzazz at Whitebrook. The horse was a big chestnut with four perfect white socks. Cassidy grabbed Melanie's arm. "Doesn't that look like Pizzazz?" she asked.

"Well, yeah, but it can't be," Melanie said. "We just saw him in the barn. Anyway, why would they be loading him on a truck?"

Cassidy pulled Melanie and Christina around to the side of a big four-wheel-drive vehicle. From there they had a good view of the groom, who loaded the horse up into the truck. A few moments later Jerry stuck his head out of the truck, looked around surreptitiously, then led a horse down the ramp. The horse was a big, energetic chestnut, with four white socks. A reddish-brown chicken followed them off, flapping and clucking as the groom shooed her out of the truck. Jerry led the horse, followed by the chicken, back toward the holding barn. As soon as the horse was off the truck, the other man quickly put away the ramp and closed the door. Then he looped a chain through the handles and padlocked it closed. With a quick look around, he hurried to the barn after the first man.

Cassidy, Melanie, and Christina looked at each other. "Did I just see what I thought I saw?" Melanie asked.

"Did you just see a groom lead Pizzazz onto a truck, lead him back off again, then padlock the door?" Cassidy asked.

Melanie nodded.

"That's what I saw," Cassidy said.

"Then we all saw the same thing," Christina said. "Boy, was that weird."

"We've got to take a look in that truck," Cassidy said. "Come on."

Looking around to be sure no one was watching, the three girls made their way between the parked cars and trucks and trailers until they reached the truck. Cassidy checked the padlock. "Locked," she said.

Christina stood by in case the groom came back, while Cassidy and Melanie went around the outside of the truck, looking for a side door. There was one, but it was also locked. All of the dark tinted windows in the truck were closed.

"Someone's coming," Christina hissed. The three girls crouched down behind another car, where they had a partial view of the back of the truck. The second groom was back again, this time carrying two buckets full of water.

"What's he doing?" Cassidy asked. They watched the groom set down the buckets and unlock the padlock. He carried the two full buckets inside. A few moments later he came out again, locking the door behind him.

"That's weird," Christina said. "Why would he be carrying water onto an empty truck?"

"Maybe it's not empty," Melanie said.

That gave Cassidy an idea. She had been searching all the sides of the truck with her eyes and had spotted what looked to be a skylight of some sort on the roof. "Do you guys think you could boost me up to the top?"

"Oh, no, not that again," Melanie groaned.

"Come on, you can stand on my shoulders," Christina said. "But take your shoes off."

Cassidy slipped off her loafers. Somehow, with a lot of giggling and wiggling, she managed to balance on Christina's shoulders long enough to stand up and pull herself onto the top of the truck. She dropped to her stomach so she'd be less likely to be seen, then pulled herself along until she reached the skylight.

It was propped open about six inches. Through it the sun shone down in a little rectangle illuminating the hindquarter of a chestnut horse.

"What do you see?" Melanie asked anxiously.

"I see a chestnut horse—I could swear it's Pizzazz," Cassidy told them.

"Except we just saw them leading Pizzazz off the truck," Christina said, puzzled. "I don't get it."

"Are we sure that was Pizzazz?" Melanie said.

"Melanie, just to make sure, can you go back to the barn and see if Pizzazz is there?" Cassidy asked. "I'm going to see if I can get this skylight open a little further." She began to work the skylight open wider.

Melanie said, "Okay. Christina, you're keeping watch in case the groom comes back, right?"

Christina nodded. Melanie went off to the holding barn. In less than two minutes she was back. "It's definitely him," she reported. "Some reporters are interviewing the owners, and they're standing right by him."

Cassidy had managed to pull the skylight open as wide as it would go. There was just room enough to stick her head in and get a good look at the horse. He was a chestnut, the same size as Pizzazz, with identical markings. But something about the way this horse carried himself was just different—they way people had different mannerisms, Cassidy thought. He might look like Pizzazz on the outside, but he wasn't Pizzazz on the inside. She took one last look and then took her head out of the opening. Then suddenly, she understood why the other horse was in the trailer.

"You guys, I know what's going on!" Cassidy said. "They must have known Pizzazz wouldn't pass the track vet's exam! So they got this other horse that looks identical to him, and they let the track vet examine him instead! No one noticed the switch. Except us," she added, pushing the skylight back to half-closed. She began to climb down from the top of the truck. "All we have to do is go tell all those reporters, and everyone will know about it! We can stop the race!"

12

CASSIDY DROPPED TO THE GROUND AND WALKED AROUND TO the back of the truck where she had left Melanie and Christina. They weren't there. "Okay, you guys, this isn't funny," she said, looking around uneasily. At least they hadn't taken her shoes. She slipped them back on. "You guys? Hey, where are you? Come on, we've got to go tell those reporters about Pizzazz's double before it's too late."

"Cassidy?" Melanie appeared from around one side of the truck. She had a strange, uncomfortable look on her face. Christina was right behind her.

"There you are," Cassidy said. "This is no time to be hiding. Come on, let's go!"

But Melanie and Christina didn't budge.

"What's the matter with you two?" Cassidy said, puzzled. "Why are you standing there like . . ." Jerry, the groom, was standing behind the two of them.

"Would you like to come over here and join your friends?" Jerry said in a chilly, polite voice. Cassidy knew he didn't expect an answer.

Melanie mouthed a word at her: "Run."

For a second she didn't budge. Then Cassidy turned and bolted toward the barn. She knew Jerry must have heard her talking. There was no telling what he would do. She had to get someone to help Melanie and Christina!

She glanced over her shoulder to see if he was following and ran right smack into someone—someone who grabbed her.

"Let me go!" she had time to shriek, before he covered her mouth with one smelly hand and dragged her, struggling and kicking, back to the truck.

Cassidy bit his hand.

"Ow!" he yelled, letting go of her mouth.

"You let us go!" Cassidy shouted. "Help!"

"Shut up, both of you," the Jerry said.

"Let me go!" Cassidy demanded.

"Let her go, Jacinto," Jerry said coolly. "She ain't going nowhere." He raised his hand to show her what was in it. It was a gun.

Cassidy stopped yelling. Jacinto let go of her, still rubbing at his hand. Was the gun real? Cassidy wasn't sure, but it looked real enough that she didn't dare to run away again.

"Open the truck, Jacinto," Jerry told him.

Jacinto took a key from his pocket and unlocked the

padlock. The chain rattled as it slid through the handles. He pulled one side of the back doors open.

"Ladies?" Jerry said, gesturing at the open door.

"What do you want us to do?" Melanie asked.

Cassidy realized what Jerry had in mind. He meant to lock them in the truck with the horse.

"Come on, get in the truck," he said impatiently. "I've got a horse to tend to."

Reluctantly the girls stepped into the truck. The chestnut horse turned around to see who was coming inside. He laid back his ears and bared his teeth at the girls as if to warn them to leave him alone, then he went back to eating from the haynet tied up in front of him.

"You're not going to leave us in here, are you?" Christina said, eyeing the surly horse.

"That's exactly what I'm going to do," Jerry said. He closed the door.

"What'll we do?" Christina said, looking panicked.

"We've got to get out of here somehow!" Cassidy said. She looked around frantically.

Jerry's voice came to them, muffled, from outside the truck. "The match race goes off in one hour. And it's going to go off. When it's over, maybe we'll think about letting you out." Cassidy heard the chain rattle as he passed it through the handles.

Locked inside the truck they would be helpless to stop the race. And, Cassidy realized, no one would be likely to come looking for them back here, no matter how loudly they yelled.

"Oh, and I wouldn't try to yell if I were you," Jerry added, as if he were reading her mind. "Red, your partner in there, he don't like yelling much. You see all those dents in the wall?"

Cassidy looked around. Sure enough, there were several hefty dents in the metal walls of the trailer where Red must have kicked out. Cassidy wasn't really too worried about the horse. She was pretty sure Jerry was just trying to scare them so they would keep quiet.

"Now you be good, girls. See you later," Jerry said, and they heard the padlock click as he locked it.

Cassidy thought about the race, feeling completely frustrated. Now she knew for sure what was going on, but there was no chance to stop it. She had failed. She thought how it would be . . . the post parade, with just the two horses. She could imagine the crowds in the grandstand and down by the rail. How they would roar when their favorite passed by. Then to the post—both the filly and the colt with their lead ponies, the colt almost cantering in place in his eagerness, the catlike filly prancing a little, daintily, because she felt good. The assistant starters would load the horses into the gate, just the two of them. There would be the momentary pause, the crowds murmuring, then the bell, the gates flying open, and the two horses, colt and filly, blazing head to head up the first furlong.

Cassidy could envision them: two perfect specimens of Thoroughbred horse, muscle and bone and blood pumping speed through their flying limbs as they sped down the track. Except one of them, Cassidy knew, was not quite perfect. One of the horses, the colt, would be galloping his heart out, betrayed by the drugs that masked the pain. He would battle the track and the filly beside him, unaware that the harder he ran, the more damage he was doing to himself—the cartilage and delicate structures in his knee being ripped ragged with every beautiful stride. Cassidy thought of Ruffian, whose leg had somehow simply snapped, and of how bewildered, and in pain, she had tried to keep running, because her heart told her it's what she was meant to do. She imagined the same thing happening to Pizzazz, his knee finally giving out, bone rubbing on bone, the pain coming at last, signaling to the confused animal that something was wrong.

There were tears in Cassidy's eyes, and she began pounding on the door. "Help!" she yelled, "Somebody help! Get us out of here, please!"

The chestnut horse, Red, gave an annoyed kick at the wall of the truck. "Cassidy, be quiet," Christina said. "There's no room to get away from him if he's goes crazy. He'll kill us all!"

"I don't care!" Cassidy cried. "We've got to get out of here! Come on, help me make some noise! Maybe someone will hear us. Do you want to just sit here and hope they come back to let us out?"

Christina and Melanie looked at each other for a second. Then all three girls began pounding on the door and yelling, making as much noise as they could. Red

160

did kick at the wall a couple of times, but they ignored him. It was helping make noise, as far as Cassidy was concerned. But after five minutes of yelling, their voices were hoarse and no one had come.

"No one's around," Melanie said. "They're all watching the races."

"Oh, no," Cassidy moaned, slumping to the floor, her back to the door. "It's going to be too late." She looked up, sadly. Then something caught her eye, and she jumped to her feet again. "The skylight!" she exclaimed.

Melanie and Christina looked up at the roof. "How are we going to get up there?" Christina asked.

"We're not," Cassidy said. "Melanie is. Come on, help me boost her up."

It wasn't easy, but somehow they helped Melanie up on Cassidy's shoulders, where she managed to crouch shakily. "Hurry up," Cassidy said, her hands on Melanie's ankles, her teeth clenched with effort.

"I'm trying," Melanie said, wrestling with the sky-light. "It's stuck."

"Can't you fit through there?" Christina asked.

"I'm little, but I'm not that little," Melanie said.

"No kidding," Cassidy said, her face red from the exertion.

"Here, put one foot on my shoulder," Christina offered.

But when Melanie tried shifting one foot, she fell, landing on the trailer floor with a thud. "Ow," Melanie said.

"Oh, Mel, are you okay?" Christina asked.

Melanie winced. "Yeah, I'm fine."

"Come on, let's try it again," Cassidy said.

This time she did a better job of placing her feet and managed to stay balanced. "Got it!" Melanie said triumphantly. She stood up, shakily, and with a last hard push off of Cassidy and Christina's shoulders, climbed through the skylight.

Cassidy rubbed her shoulder as she watched Melanie's feet disappear up through the opening. A second later they were replaced by Melanie's head. "I'm going for help," she said. "Be back as fast as I can."

"Hurry up," Christina said. "It's stuffy in here with all these warm bodies."

Her head disappeared, then reappeared in the opening. "Stay right here," Melanie joked.

"Melanie!" Christina and Cassidy said at the same time.

"Okay, okay, I'm going," Melanie said. This time her head disappeared for good.

Christina and Cassidy sat on the trailer floor, waiting for Melanie to bring help. Both girls were silent. The only noise in the trailer came from Red, who kept up a continuous swishing of his long, thick tail. Cassidy thought she was going to climb the walls if she didn't get out of the trailer. "It's so hot in here," she said.

"No wonder Red's so ornery," Christina said.

Then they heard a sound from outside. "Anybody in there?" a familiar voice said.

Cassidy's head shot up. "Charlie?" she said.

"Who's that?" Charlie McGowan said.

"Charlie!" the girls yelled, jumping to their feet. "It's us! Charlie, you've got to get us out of here!"

"Hang on, I'll have you out in a minute," he promised.

There was a loud bang against the door, then two more. On the fourth one, Cassidy heard the chain slide through the handles. She was pushing the door open almost before the chain was completely off.

"How in the world did you three get locked in here?" he asked.

"Didn't Melanie tell you?" Cassidy asked.

Charlie shook his head. "She just told me where to find you, then she said she had to go get Ashleigh."

"Never mind," Cassidy said. "We'll tell you later. Where's Pizzazz?"

Charlie glanced at his watch. "Well, it's about fifteen minutes to post time," he said. "They came for Lady T about ten minutes ago. I imagine by now the colt's over in the paddock, too."

"Then we've still got time," Cassidy said. She ran back into the truck and began untying Pizzazz's twin, Red. He bared his teeth and snapped at her when she first came near him, but she ignored his antics. "Come on, Red," Cassidy said. "You've got an important job to do today." When she had him untied, she turned him around and led him off the truck. Once she had him in hand he behaved himself just fine.

163

"Let's go," Cassidy said.

"Where are we going?" Charlie asked. "And what are you doing with that horse? He sure looks like Pizzazz, doesn't he?"

"To the paddock, quick," Cassidy said.

"Now hold on here," Charlie said. "I'm not going anywhere until you tell me what this is all about." He folded his arms and looked from Christina to Cassidy expectantly.

Quickly they explained what was happening. After that, Charlie needed no coaxing.

Cassidy clucked at Red to get him to move on, and the two girls, escorted by Charlie, hurried behind the barn toward the paddock area, the chestnut horse trotting along with them.

"Charlie, what time is it?" Cassidy asked.

Charlie glanced at his watch. "It's ten minutes to post time," he said. "Don't worry, you've still got time." He was huffing and puffing, but he jogged along gamely. When they got to the holding barn, Jerry stepped into their path, blocking their way.

"Where do you think you're taking that horse?" he shouted.

13

"OUT OF THE WAY, PLEASE," CHARLIE SAID IN A VOICE THAT most people wouldn't have argued with.

"Now what makes you think you can order me around?" Jerry said, one hand behind his back.

"This," Charlie said drawing his gun.

"Charlie, watch out," Cassidy cautioned. "He's got a gun, too. He's the one who locked us up."

"Bring your hand around real slow and drop your weapon," Charlie ordered.

Jerry did it, but there was something funny in his expression. Cassidy looked behind them just in time to see Jacinto sneaking up. "Charlie, behind you, look out!" she yelled.

Charlie stepped back just as Jerry lunged for him. But to Cassidy's surprise, Christina jumped forward and tackled Jerry. "Hey!" he cried out in surprise. He was six inches shorter than Christina, who also out-weighed him by a few pounds. She had no trouble knocking him down.

"Good going, kid," Charlie said, picking up Jerry's gun.

"Thanks," Christina said.

"You can get up," Charlie told Christina, who cautiously climbed off of Jerry. "You stay right there," he said to Jerry, who was still on his stomach where he had fallen. "And you get right down there with him," he said, gesturing with his gun to Jacinto, who quickly complied. "You kids go on to the paddock," he told the girls. "Let me take care of these guys." He took out his walkie-talkie and began calling for more security guards, while he kept a wary eye on the two grooms.

"Right," Cassidy said. "Come on, hurry. There isn't much time."

The girls ran to the paddock, leading the horse. The steward on duty there looked puzzled when he saw the horse, but he still wouldn't let them into the paddock area.

"You've got to let us through!" Cassidy said.

He shook his head. "I'm sorry, but I can't do that. You can come in; you have a paddock pass. But you can't bring this horse through here."

Cassidy was beginning to panic. There couldn't be more than a few minutes left before the race. "You don't understand," she pleaded with the steward. "We've got to get this horse in there. You've got to let us through."

"Christina, Cassidy!" someone was calling.

They both turned around. "Mom!" Christina said.

"Hi, Ashleigh," the steward said.

Ashleigh and Melanie hurried to join them. "Are you two all right?" Ashleigh said, looking gravely at the two girls. "Melanie told me what happened. You're not hurt, are you?"

"No," Christina said. "But we have to get through here! We have to get this horse into the paddock so everyone can see him. They've been using him as a ringer for Pizzazz!"

"Billy," Ashleigh said to the steward. "Let them in please."

He crossed his arms stubbornly. "I'm not supposed to—"

"Go on, girls," Ashleigh urged them.

"Go," Christina said, giving Cassidy a little shove.

"Hey," Billy said. "You can't just—"

But Cassidy wasn't going to wait to hear what he had to say. She figured Ashleigh would handle it. She tugged on Red and he followed her through the paddock gate.

People thronged the area surrounding the paddock where the jockeys mounted up, and horses could be viewed before the race. Television cameras on booms recorded the commotion from above the crowds. Cassidy ran right into the paddock, with Red, toward the first reporter she spotted with a camera. "Stop the race!"

she yelled loudly. "You have to stop the race!"

All the cameras swung toward her. The crowd grew quiet, then loud again with urgent murmuring when they saw the girl with the horse that was a ringer for the famous colt, Pizzazz.

"Cassidy!" she heard someone say, and it sounded like her dad but she couldn't tell where the voice had come from. Several people held microphones toward Cassidy as she told everyone what was going on as rapidly and clearly as she could. ". . . because his knee is in such bad shape. So the track vet really examined this horse," Cassidy said. "They used him because they knew if he examined Pizzazz, he wouldn't pass the exam or the drug test. Pizzazz isn't fit to run."

There was an uneasy silence in the crowd after she spoke. Then Cassidy caught sight of her parents standing near Lady T in the area where the jockeys mounted up. Her mother looked stunned, while her father just gazed calmly at her. Cassidy couldn't read his expression.

"I'm sorry, Dad," Cassidy said. "I know this means you could lose Lady T. And I know I might lose my horses, too."

"Lose your horses?" Christina asked her.

Cassidy nodded.

"Wow," Christina said softly.

Cassidy went on, "But I just couldn't stand for Pizzazz to get hurt. It's not right." Her voice trembled a little, but she kept it level as she went on speaking.

"People shouldn't just use animals to make money when it's going to hurt the animal."

Then the reporters started talking a mile a minute, some questioning her intently, some talking into microphones and cameras. Cassidy saw Ashleigh talking with the track stewards and knew she was confirming what Cassidy had told them. Someone shoved a microphone at Cassidy, but she pushed it aside and ignoring all the questions, stood holding Red, her eyes on her father.

Harrison Smith left the area where he had been standing and slowly walked toward the center of the paddock, cameras following. He stood in silence, facing his daughter.

Cassidy waited to hear what he would say. Finally he spoke, turning to face the cameras. "There will be no match race," Harrison Smith announced.

The people began to murmur again. Reporters were firing questions at Cassidy and her dad, but they didn't answer. Cassidy simply stared into her father's green eyes, searching for some response to what she had done. She was hoping for forgiveness, but she wasn't at all sure she would find it. A tear rolled down her cheek, and then another, while she waited.

Harrison Smith ignored all the cameras and microphones. After what seemed like an eternity, he spoke. "You did the right thing, Cassidy," he said simply. Slowly he reached out and put an arm around his daughter. Then he escorted her out of the paddock area.

As they made their way through the crowd, the people stepped back, opening up a path. Then someone began to clap. In a moment, the applause became thunderous.

Once Cassidy glimpsed Ashleigh's face in the crowd. Ashleigh smiled at her and gave her an encouraging nod.

"You're awesome, Cassidy," she heard Melanie say.

The tears blurred Cassidy's eyes and she stumbled along, but her father's strong arm across her shoulders steadied her.

"You did the right thing," he said again, and hugged her with the same arm.

Cassidy squeezed him back, her arm around his waist. She thought of her horses, Rebound and Wellington, and of Pizzazz, and of Lady T. She remembered what Mona had said about heart. Tears kept pouring from her eyes and she felt sadder than she had ever felt, but at the same time she was elated. She didn't know what would happen now, but in her heart, she knew she had made the right choice.

ALLISON ESTES grew up in Oxford, Mississippi. She first sat on a horse when she was four years old, got a pony when she was ten, and has been riding horses ever since. Ms. Estes lives in New York City and works as a trainer at Claremont Riding Academy. She plays on four softball teams, and, between games, has written over a dozen other books for young readers.

THOROUGHBRED

If you enjoyed this book, then you'll love reading all the books in the THOROUGHBRED series!

www.harpercollins.com